SCHOOL FOR SLEUTHS

SCHOOL FOR SLEUTHS

DAN ANDRIACCO

WILDSIDE PRESS

This book is lovingly dedicated to
Beth Andriacco
and she knows why

ONE

"WE CLEAN UP CRIME ON THE CHEAP"

The prospective client spoke in a rush, as if to purge himself of the distasteful words: "I think my stepmother killed my father."

"I see," said the man behind the desk, his full-moon face suffused with sympathy. He was short, with hair receding in front and thinning at the crown. "That's a very serious charge. Do you have any evidence?"

"Nothing hard. I can't even prove it's murder. That's why I want to hire a detective, Mr. Finn."

Francis Aloysius Finn, the owner and only full-time employee of the agency that early morning in the summer of 1991, allowed himself a circumspect smile. He reveled in the prospect of a meaty case and a client who, from the looks of him, was the sort of individual A-Plus was designed to serve.

Squirming in Finn's imitation leather chair, Norris Beamer was dressed in the standard uniform of the upper middle class: khaki slacks, snazzy blue blazer, red and blue rep tie. A fortyish accountant, Finn guessed—or maybe a sales rep. The blazer was unbuttoned in the inadequately cooled office.

"I'll just take a few notes while you fill me in on your father's death," Finn said as he drew a yellow legal pad from his middle desk drawer. "My secretary had a nervous breakdown and I'm still waiting for the temp agency to send me a replacement."

Beamer eyed the tile floor and scuffed walls of the cubicle office. "You know, I only picked this agency because it's the first one listed in the Yellow Pages. I was surprised to find you located in a strip center between a florist and a video store."

"I like to keep my overhead down. It reduces the cost to you." From the jumble on a corner of his desk Finn handed Beamer a yellow plastic litter bag shaped like a gun holster. On the top it said

"A-Plus Detective Agency & Famous Detectives School." Below was Finn's motto: "We clean up crime on the cheap."

Beamer tried to give it back.

"Keep it." Finn waved his hand. "I have plenty of advertising specialties. Always send away for the free samples. You want a fly swatter? Maybe a rain bonnet for the wife?"

"I'm not married anymore," Beamer protested. "Listen, I'm really not sure your firm—"

"Believe me, Mr. Beamer, you'll feel a lot better once you tell me all about it." Finn uncapped a felt-tipped pen.

"Well, since I'm already here..." Beamer dropped the litter bag on the floor by his chair. "Where do you want me to start?"

"Tell me why you suspect foul play," Finn said, "and why you think your stepmother is behind it."

"For one thing, why would she have the body cremated if not to destroy any evidence of murder? I'm sure my father intended to be buried. He owned a burial plot right next to my mom."

"Maybe he changed his mind about using it. Would your father have discussed a thing like that with you? Were you close?"

Beamer studied the shoe laces at the end of his crossed legs. "Not in some time."

"Because of your father's remarriage?" This was looking like familiar ground to Finn—an adult child, still mourning his mother's demise and ready to cast the new wife as the evil stepmother from a Grimm's fairy tale.

Beamer stuck a menthol cigarette in his mouth, just under the dishwater blond mustache crawling across his upper lip. "My father's remarriage had nothing to do with it. He only met this woman last year; we were estranged long before that. Mind if I smoke?"

Finn himself indulged in too-expensive cigars when he was deep in thought on a case. He opened a side drawer in his desk and pulled out a dented metal ash tray emblazoned with "A-Plus Detective Agency" in black and the motto "We're hot on the trail" in red. He handed it to the client.

Beamer lit up and inhaled. He seemed to want to talk. "My father, Otto Beamer, was seventy-four years old and stubborn as they come, Mr. Finn. Wouldn't take any advice, especially financial. We fought about money constantly. It came to a head a couple of years ago when I tried to talk him into cashing in his stocks and putting the proceeds into my savings and loan, where it would be safe. I'm the branch manager at Old Colonial S&L in Westwood."

"An S&L? That's safe?"

"We're a very sound institution, I guarantee you, Mr. Finn. We're not like all those thrifts that have failed in recent years here in Ohio. But Pop flew into a rage and accused me of trying to get his money before he was even dead." Beamer kept his eyes on the ash of his cigarette. "I was an only child."

"And you hadn't talked to your father since that argument?"

"No. He didn't even invite me to his wedding, not that I would have gone. And after he died last week I found out that he'd cut me out of his will and left everything to that, that *beast* he married—even my mother's things."

"As his wife—"

"The woman's in her mid-fifties and looks ten years younger. A hot number. When I first saw her at the funeral home she was laughing. Not twenty feet from the body. Do you think she married a man well into his seventies for love or romance? Or even sex?"

Finn, although a life-long bachelor, was not one to discount the possibility. He set down his pen. "I can see why you're upset, Mr. Beamer, but you haven't said anything yet that points to homicide."

Beamer uncrossed his legs. "Then consider this: My father was never sick a day in his life. He walked five miles every day and his hair was still more black than gray. Yet supposedly he died of a heart attack. There was no autopsy and the body was cremated. Viola—that's my stepmother—is a nurse at the Hanging Gardens Retirement Center. Wouldn't she know how to do away with an old man without making it obvious?"

"Maybe," Finn conceded. "But surprise heart attacks, even fatal ones, aren't uncommon at that age. Have you gone to the police with this?"

Beamer nodded. "Several times. Without results. I suspect the police think I'm just a greedy son trying to make trouble because I was written out of the will."

"I wouldn't be surprised. You didn't give them anything to justify an investigation—unless you've forgotten to tell me something."

Beamer exhaled smoke through his nostrils. "My father had a hundred thousand dollars in life insurance. Viola got that, too. With the house and my parents' life savings, she'll walk away with close to two hundred and fifty thousand."

"Do you know the name of the insurer?"

"Cheviot Mutual Insurance. I'd been urging my father to drop them for years. I hear they're the cheapest people in the business."

Finn couldn't argue with that. Cheviot Mutual's legendary parsimony had made the firm a frequent client of the A-Plus Detective Agency in these early months of operation. He had an unclosed fraud case for the company right now. Although he would rather work for individuals, Finn couldn't yet afford to turn down good fees for investigating insurance claims. Not that the fees were princely, especially from Cheviot Mutual. He found it hard to believe that tightfisted outfit would ever pay out a life claim for a hundred thousand dollars without thoroughly checking it out first.

"I doubt that there's a murder case here, Mr. Beamer," Finn said. "Not one that we can prove, anyway. The lack of a body makes it pretty dicey."

Beamer began to rise from his chair.

"But let me tell you what might be easier to prove," Finn added quickly. "Incompetence or undue influence."

Years of working as an investigator for the prosecuting attorney's office and a year of night law school had given Finn an air of authority in delivering legal terms. Beamer sat back down.

"Is this going to get me my inheritance back?"

"If we can prove that your father was incompetent when he made his will, or that he was unduly influenced by your stepmother, then the document is invalid, and you inherit as the next of kin. You'll need a lawyer to fight that for you, but we can handle the investigation. First, however, I need considerably more information about your father and his second wife."

For thirty minutes Beamer talked and smoked while Finn took notes. The detective learned that Otto Beamer had been a retired IRS employee whose first wife, Norris's mother, had died sixteen years ago. He had met Viola Rosselli, a widow, nine months previously at a senior citizens' Halloween party. The couple had married at Christmas. By the fourth of July, Viola was once again a widow.

After collecting details about Otto's friends (the few who were still alive), neighbors, and lifelong habits, Finn pushed aside his yellow legal pad. "That's a start. By this time next week, I'll know more about Viola Rosselli Beamer than she knows about herself. I'll have my staff excavate her background, talk to the neighbors about how she treated your father, even probe her trash for deep secrets."

Beamer looked around the office. "What staff? You don't even have a secretary."

"Let me assure you, sir," Finn said, rising to his full five-foot-four, "a secretary is on order. As for the investigators, they're provided by our Famous Detectives School."

"School? You mean a bunch of *students* are going to be handling my case? A murder?" Beamer's voice was as weak as his mustache.

"I prefer to think of them as interns, detectives in training. They pay me tuition to learn the craft of sleuthing, and I give them field experience as well as a rigorous course of lectures by myself and other experts. It's on-the-job training. Doctors do it; teachers do it; why not detectives?"

Norris Beamer sat open-mouthed.

"Naturally," Finn continued, "this arrangement keeps labor costs low. And that, Mr. Beamer, is why the services of our school for sleuths will cost you only half of what any other investigative agency in town would charge. It's like getting a haircut at a barber college—a real bargain."

"If I don't get clipped," the client muttered.

TWO

"DREAMER, SCHEMER, ROMANTIC, AND ROGUE"

Such skepticism frequently meets the dreams of visionaries, and Francis Aloysius Finn was a visionary of the detective business.

A mere three months earlier, Finn was an investigator in the Hamilton County prosecutor's office. He had worked there for twenty-five years and thought he always would. Then came the budget crunch and the downsizing under a new prosecutor. Finn was out of a job for the first time in his life. What to do? The answer was easy, thanks to the counsel, years before, of his late father.

Michael Terrence "Mickey" Finn had been a printer. But his hobby was arranging flowers and he long harbored a secret ambition to own a small flower shop. He never told anyone, not even his wife and son, until those last weeks of his life. With the cancer eating away at his body, he looked back with regret at the dream unrealized.

"You've got to follow your passion, Frank," he told his son. "It's the only way to be happy in this life."

In the five years since, Finn slowly came to the realization that while investigative work was his passion, doing it for somebody else wasn't. He wanted to build his own detective business—a kind the world had never seen. He could offer bargain rates and train new detectives at the same time. But, like his father before him, he never had the guts to leave a secure job to do it.

When the job turned out to be not so secure, it was like a liberation. With his father's advice as his inspiration and his severance pay for capital, Finn hired a secretary, leased cheap space and cheaper furniture, and had stationery printed. He was in business. Dad would be proud of him from heaven.

Not that business was booming. In fact, Finn wasn't getting enough cases to give all his students the practical experience he'd promised. Maybe that's why Joe Canova had blown a simple stakeout. It was definitely why Finn's monthly bills were exceeding his cash flow. He couldn't make it on student fees alone with the number of students he had; he needed clients.

Even with Norris Beamer's check in his pocket as a retainer, therefore, Finn was drawn to the *Queen City Courier* for his customary perusal of the crime news in small type in the back pages. He opened the suburban weekly as soon as Beamer left. No telling what transgression described there might become a case for the A-Plus Detective Agency if only the victim were properly approached about the need for the firm's services.

But, alas, the only item to stir even a flicker of interest in Finn's watery gray eyes was a petty crime notable only for the villain's abominable taste:

> Theft. July 9 at 4620 Meisendorf Road. Statue
> of Sleepy the Dwarf stolen from front yard;
> value, $100; one of a set of seven.

Of course it was one of seven, Finn thought to himself. It didn't take a Sherlock Holmes to figure out that the other six were Dopey, Sneezy, Grumpy, Bashful, Doc, and... and...

In disgust Finn tossed the newspaper into the waste basket at the side of his desk, intending to embark on a further examination of the new Victoria's Secret catalog in his top drawer. But as he bent over, he heard the sound of a female voice calling his name. He went out to meet his visitor.

She was in her late thirties, an age that Finn—at forty-six himself—found enormously appealing. She must have stood about five-foot-eleven, but looked taller because of her flawless posture and the way her wheat-colored hair kissed the tops of her shoulders. Her navy blue suit and crisp white blouse made Finn feel comparatively grungy in his rumpled pinstripes. She wore simple pearl earrings, possibly natural rather than cultured. The platinum and diamond rings on her left hand seemed expensive, but by no means gaudy.

A class act, this woman, rather like that model in the black lace teddy on page four of the Victoria's Secret catalog. She was not at all the sort of person who would have a skull tattooed on her forearm, Finn was quite sure.

"Mr. Finn?" Her eyes were wide and violet and intelligent.

Words failing him, Finn could only nod assent.

She stuck out her hand. "My name is Mrs. Hilary Kendrake." The firmness of her handshake surprised him. "I'm the secretary from Office Temps."

Finn straightened his red tie. "And not a moment too soon, madam. My need for a secretary is becoming critical. Can you complete the following sequence: Sleepy, Dopey, Sneezy, Grumpy, Bashful, Doc, and…?"

"Happy," she said, a look of consternation on her face belying the word.

Finn smiled. "Welcome aboard. Let me show you around the A-Plus Detective Agency." He gestured with both arms at the surrounding room with its Formica-topped desk, a row of plastic chairs against the opposite wall, and a table laden with month-old news magazines. He wished he'd had the cracks in the walls patched before he moved in. "This is our reception area. We aren't busy right now."

She arched an eyebrow. "So it seems."

"Someday, though, the A-Plus Detective Agency & Famous Detectives School is going to be the H&R Block, the Hyatt Legal Services of the detective business. I'm talking about affordable sleuths for Mid-America, Mrs. Kendrake. Franchises in every city in our country!"

Hilary Kendrake—such a nice name!—leveled her wide eyes at Finn. "Do you really think there's that much of a market for cheap detectives?"

"Of course! The public just doesn't know it yet. You don't suppose everybody thought McDonald's was such a hot idea before that first Mcburger was flipped, do you? By no means! It took marketing, Mrs. Kendrake. That's why I gave this agency a name that placed it first in the Yellow Pages listing of private investigators—marketing. And that strategy brought me a new client only this morning. A possible homicide, although I doubt we can prove it."

"You could have called the company AA, just for good measure."

Finn shook his head. "I don't drink that much. Besides, I like the 'plus.' It has the ring of something extra special."

He took Kendrake back into his own office. He pointed out the antique cherry desk, the woodgrain file cabinet, the bookcase full of true crime and crime reference books, the phone with six separate lines (going nowhere), the small refrigerator stocked with Snickers bars and other snacks, the Currier & Ives prints on the wall that had previously graced last year's calendar.

When Finn caught her looking at the holster-shaped litter bag left on the tile floor by Norris Beamer, he bent to pick it up.

"Do you carry a gun?" Kendrake asked.

Everybody asked private eyes that, even beautiful ladies.

"I don't like firearms," Finn said with a smile.

"I hate them, too. But I carry mace on my key chain, next to a Swiss Army knife."

Cautious woman.

Finn pressed on, showing her the two similar but smaller offices behind his own. "Any student in the school can use them for interviews, or homework, or just plain taking a nap."

"I've never been in a private detective's office, I must admit, but this seems like an odd physical setup for this kind of business."

"That's a holdover from the former tenant," Finn explained. "These cubicles were patient examining rooms."

"This was a doctor's office?"

"A vet's, actually. I'm still working on getting all the animal hair out." He made a mental note to get on that.

Across the hallway, one big room ran parallel to the three rooms on the left. Wooden folding chairs, the kind you'd sit in under the bingo tent at a church festival, were lined up in rows. A blackboard was mounted on the wall at the front of the room.

"This is the classroom for our Famous Detectives School," Finn said, pride in his voice. "Do you understand how we work?"

"I've been briefed." Kendrake swung the hair off her shoulders with a graceful movement. "Your students learn the detective trade by investigating cases for the A-Plus Detective Agency. So you really have two synergistic businesses here. You get paid from both ends, sort of like the credit card companies."

What a charming, insightful woman, Finn thought.

"Let me warn you," he said as they walked toward the back of the building, "the storage room is a disaster area."

This was no exaggeration. The room had no furniture except for a large, Formica-topped table and three or four plastic chairs. What it did have lots of was paper—incoming mail, outgoing mail, and stacks of eight-and-a-half-by-eleven-inch sheets.

"We're running a little behind on the mail order operation," Finn explained.

"Mail order?"

"You haven't you seen our ad on matchbook covers, then?"

"I'm afraid not. I don't smoke."

Finn produced a pack of matches from his right vest pocket. He held it open for Kendrake to read the inside cover:

Do you have what it takes to be a

PRIVATE EYE?

You could be the next Jim Rockford or Magnum, PI. But you may never know for sure unless you take the free aptitude test from the

FAMOUS DETECTIVES SCHOOL

Absolutely no obligation!

Approved for veterans

There was a little picture of Humphrey Bogart in a fedora hat, and below that a coupon to fill out and send away for the test.

"A correspondence school for detectives?" Kendrake said.

"It's the same course we give down the hallway. The only difference is the field work. Mail order students have to pick that up on their own."

"How many respondents have failed this free aptitude test?"

Finn shook his head. "I don't believe in failure, Mrs. Kendrake. With good instruction anyone can become a detective, and it's my role to see that they do." This philosophy was being sorely tested by more than one student of the Famous Detectives School, but Finn kept that to himself.

Kendrake crossed her arms and smiled. "Dreamer, schemer, romantic, and rogue."

"Pardon?"

"That's how Leopold Pope described you."

Finn narrowed his eyes. "How do you know old 'Pope Leopold'?"

"He's my uncle. My late husband's uncle, really."

Pope Leopold's nephew! Finn remembered the tragic story with the force of a physical blow. The young man had been Leopold's law partner, almost as well-known and respected as his venerable mentor. He had been shot down on the courthouse steps by a madman upset over a divorce ruling in Domestic Relations Court. The dead man's ex-wife, Finn seemed to remember, had been slightly wounded in the melee. Perhaps that was why Mrs. Kendrake made a point of saying she hated guns. How long ago had the shooting been—four years? Five? Time passed with such frightening swiftness these days.

"I used to work in their office," Kendrake added, "but I've been out of the work force for some years. I'm easing back in with temporary work. Uncle Leopold told me about you when I got this assignment from Office Temps. It sounded like an interesting position. But what exactly are my duties? I warn you, I don't make coffee."

"Do you condescend to do mail? There's a month's worth to be answered here." Finn gestured around the room. "But wait, never mind that. We can always blame the Post Office if the lessons don't go out on time. There's more urgent work to be done in my office."

Kendrake followed him back down the hallway, where Finn pointed to the stack of papers on his desk.

"What we have here are unfiled reports," he explained. "This agency lives on the accuracy of the field reports, so I insist that all my students write detailed accounts of every interview, every surveillance, every tedious hour spent going over public records in some stuffy government office. Eventually they all are copied for the client and the originals filed."

"You don't computerize that sort of thing? I've been trained on WordPerfect, WordStar, and MultiMate."

"Do you see a computer? Oh, I had one, but it was repossessed after a financial misunderstanding with the IBM people."

"You really do need help."

Kendrake lifted two stapled pages off the top of the stack and read aloud.

"'Investigator followed subject to the Rat's Nest, a sleazy little bar on the seamy side of Cincinnati's soft underbelly. It was as dark as a divorce lawyer's soul. The women didn't have teeth and the men didn't mind.'" Kendrake frowned. Finn couldn't blame her. "'Investigator bought a pitcher of Hudy Delight at the bar and carried it to a table. To investigator's consternation, subject joined him at the table and ordered a round of drinks, the first of several. Subject drank like a German sailor on the third day of a three-day pass. In order to maintain pretext, investigator was forced to do likewise. The evening went like a thief in the night, leaving investigator hazy on details.'"

Kendrake looked up. "Your student detective got soused, Mr. Finn."

Finn shut his eyes in mortification. The case was an apparent insurance scam, with A-Plus retained by Cheviot Mutual's property and casualty arm to prove that a man named Adams was faking a back injury. Finn thought that even Joe Canova could handle this one. Canova was a fireman who dreamed of being both a private eye and a private-eye writer. His novels (unpublished and probably unpublishable) were written with all the verve of a VCR manual. His investigative reports, on the other hand, sounded like bad Mickey Spillane imitations and always came in late.

"One of our less promising students," Finn commented.

To make matters worse, Canova had an unrequited crush on one of Finn's best students, Rosalee Chandler, and clearly harbored a hopeless ambition to impress her with his sleuthing prowess.

"On second thought, the filing can wait, too," Finn said. "I want to dictate some notes."

For the next forty-five minutes, Finn sat at his desk rattling off notes from the meeting that morning with Norris Beamer.

"What do you think really happened to Mr. Beamer's father?" Kendrake asked at the end.

Finn shrugged. "My mind is open. I'd love to prove murder—think of the publicity!—but I have a sneaking suspicion the client would be happy if we just managed to break the will. Whether that woman killed her husband or not, it's entirely possible that she married him to get her hands on his cushy federal pension while he was alive and the inheritance and insurance later."

Kendrake shook her head. "I suppose it's naïve of me to be shocked that someone would be so mercenary about a thing as important as marriage."

"Personally, Mrs. Kendrake, I could only marry for love." And maybe that's my problem, Finn added to himself.

"The next job," he said out loud, "is lecture notes. We've had crooks and cops and a police reporter in to give the spiel, but usually I do it myself. It's important to get it right, because the lecture notes are also the lessons for the mail order course, which is still a work in progress. And when I've finished the last lesson and put it all together, it's going to be a manual. Then comes the video cassette version—maybe a whole series. When we get franchised, every office will have the benefit of me on tape."

"When is the next class?" Kendrake asked, flipping a page in her steno book.

"Tonight. I hope you can type fast."

THREE

CLASS WORK

"In summary," Finn told his student sleuths that night, "let me reiterate that there are certain items you must have with you on a stakeout. A tape recorder, a notepad, a camera, sunglasses, binoculars, spare change, snacks, and maps are important. But if you don't have that wide-mouthed plastic bottle with you on a car stakeout, you are *dead*. It's the only way you can relieve your bladder without leaving your post. And you must not leave your post!"

A stout, white-haired woman in the back row made a note on a white pad with wide lines.

What am I doing in this place? Hilary Kendrake asked herself. *I should be home with my little girl.*

No, that wasn't true. Kendrake loved Amanda dearly, but she had hardly been out of the eight-year-old's sight, except during school hours, since Bob's murder. It was time to branch out. That was the whole idea of Kendrake finally going back to work, although at a temporary job with a minimum commitment and maximum flexibility of working hours.

And what a strange job it had turned out to be! She found herself secretary to a pint-sized private eye with delusions of empire. But it was hard not to be affected by Finn's enthusiasm, whether focused on his vision for a nationwide chain of McTective agencies or on the art of the stakeout. He hadn't asked her to come tonight, and she wasn't being paid for it, but she wanted to see this detective school in action.

The content of the lecture was no surprise—Kendrake had typed it herself on Finn's IBM Selectric II typewriter (accompanied by the detective's unreassuring promise to buy a computer again once he had straightened out his dispute with IBM and the Credit Bureau.) But Finn's delivery, peppered with impromptu anecdotes from his own career, turned an academic monologue into good theater.

"Any questions about the techniques employed in surveillance and stakeouts?" he asked at the end.

From the dozen or so students on their wooden chairs, one hand went up. It belonged to the elderly woman who was such an ardent note-taker.

"Yes, Mrs. Pertwee?" Finn said, sounding resigned as he wiped his balding head with a handkerchief.

Finn had described Mrs. Alice Pertwee to Kendrake as a retired English teacher suffering from what he called "Jessica Fletcher Syndrome." He gave her high marks for writing excellent reports, clear and to the point.

"Mr. Finn," she said in a firm but high-pitched voice, "how does a woman use that plastic bottle? There would seem to be certain, er, physical difficulties."

Finn blanched and cleared his throat as the other students guffawed. "Yes, I see what you mean. I have two recommendations in that regard, Mrs. Pertwee, based on the experience of female detectives I have known: Wear a skirt. Don't wear underwear."

Mrs. Pertwee's pen flew across her pad as she wrote down this critical advice.

After the chuckles and the snickers subsided, Finn fielded questions about the appropriate snack (he favored trail mix) and how to quench one's thirst without dangerously overloading the wide-mouth plastic bottle later (suck on ice chips).

"And now," Finn said, beginning to pace in front of the blackboard, "let me acquaint you with the facts of our latest case. The client thinks it's murder."

Concisely, but with some element of drama, Finn related the story of Otto Beamer's unexpected death and his son's suspicions of homicide. Finn made it clear that A-Plus's task was to prove murder or, failing that, at least undue influence by Viola Beamer on the writing of her late husband's will.

"Anybody have any ideas on how we should go about it?" Finn asked at the conclusion.

Hands shot up around the room.

"Yes, Mr. Mobarry?"

Finn pointed to a triple-bellied man in the first row whose raised hand was practically in Finn's face. From the class list in front of her, Kendrake identified him as Dick Mobarry, based on Finn's description. ("Our black student, Shadd Davis, calls him Moby Dick because he's big and he's white.")

"Put a phone tap on the woman," Mobarry said. "Sooner or later, she's bound to spill to somebody. I'd be glad to handle the setup."

"Your customary enthusiasm for electronic surveillance is misplaced this time, Mr. Mobarry," Finn said. "Not only would it be illegal, but—even worse—it would be premature. There's not much point in eavesdropping unless you know what to listen for. And I don't share your optimism about a convenient confession."

"Big mistake," Mobarry muttered, slouching in his seat.

Finn called on Davis, whose hand was also raised.

"A tail, man, that's what we need. I'll follow the lady till she returns to the scene of the crime."

With his hair in dreadlocks, Davis looked like a street musician who played the saxophone for spare change—which he was. Kendrake couldn't imagine him following someone without being noticed, except maybe in California.

"Mr. Beamer died at home," Finn said. "His widow lives at the scene of the crime, if there was one. However, do you have access to a truck, Mr. Davis? A four-by-four would do."

"My brother has one. But you can't follow nobody in a truck."

"I had in mind a different assignment for you," Finn said. "Remember Lesson Four?"

Davis groaned. "Oh, no, man. Not the garbage gig!"

"Precisely." Finn beamed, pleased. "I want you to go into Mrs. Beamer's neighborhood early on trash collection day and pick up her cans. Make sure you don't miss any. Then I'll show you how to sort through them for evidence about her lifestyle. Is she living with a man? Has she been subscribing to *Poison Today* magazine? You know the drill. And don't forget to wear gloves."

Davis shook his head. "Oh, *man*," he said, followed by several other words, mostly short.

"I'll handle the surveillance," asserted a male student in his early thirties. He had curly dark hair covering both his head and the arms sticking out of his short sleeve shirt.

Finn glowered. "You already have an assignment, Mr. Canova. Or have your forgotten that insurance fraud case for Cheviot Mutual?" Canova folded his arms and sat back in his chair with a look of disgust. "Besides," Finn continued, "we have no reason yet to believe that surveillance is called for. We need to know more about our target."

A young woman with shoulder-length auburn hair gathered in a barrette raised her hand.

"Yes, Ms. Chandler?" Finn said with a broad smile. That would be Rosalee Chandler, a librarian at the main branch of the Public Library of Cincinnati and Hamilton County. And obviously a teacher's pet, Kendrake noted.

"Shouldn't we do a paper chase on Mrs. Beamer?" Chandler asked. "That might turn up something in her background."

"Excellent idea," Finn praised. "Make that your assignment, Ms. Chandler. The subject's stepson knows next to nothing about her, so I want the works—where and when she was born, where she was educated, her employment history, details of her previous marriage."

"Right."

"Now, one more thing," Finn said. Hands on his hips, he surveyed the classroom. Kendrake was sure he was sizing up various students' suitability for an assignment as his eyes touched on each one. Mrs. Pertwee? Finn didn't linger there. He looked a little longer, if Kendrake followed his line of sight correctly, at a six-foot-tall woman with spikey black hair. That would be Mary Sue Barkeloo, by process of elimination. That was the only other female name on the class register.

Barkeloo, about twenty-two years old, was chewing bubble gum and batting her eyes in the direction of "Moby Dick" Mobarry. Kendrake suspected that Finn's attention had less to do with her accomplishments as a student sleuth than with the way she stuffed (or rather, didn't entirely stuff) her considerable endowments into a halter top.

Finn focused elsewhere and a smile of satisfaction stole across his face.

"Mr. Funderburgh!"

"Yes, Mr. Finn?" Funderburgh proved to be a distinguished-looking gentleman, pushing seventy, with a trim body, silver hair, and a British military mustache.

"You," said Finn, "are just the person to pay a call on the late Mr. Beamer's neighbors."

FOUR

GOOD NEIGHBORS

As he walked down the suburban street the next morning, Nelson Funderburgh felt ten years younger—maybe twenty.

He never failed to get in a day of walking since retiring from his forty-seven years as a letter carrier, but this was different. This was walking with a purpose again. He hadn't realized how much his retirement had been devoid of mission until he unexpectedly acquired one. Enrolling in this school for sleuths had been the merest lark, an amusing alternative to senior citizens' meetings where, as an eligible bachelor, he was much in demand, and summer re-runs on TV. Little had the life-long reader of mystery novels dreamed that on a hot Thursday morning in mid-July he would be sauntering down this pleasant if unremarkable street of two-story brick and aluminum houses on a *caper*.

It was the sort of neighborhood that inspired the old joke about the inebriated suburbanite fumbling at the door of the wrong residence, so much did these homes resemble each other. The chief distinction seemed to be colors—here a red brick, there a yellow one, with the occasional blue shutter instead of black.

The Beamer homestead, where the presumably merry widow still lived, was at 823 Cherry Tree Lane. (There were no cherry trees in sight.) Funderburgh planned to talk with neighbors on either side, using a pretext, to learn what he could about the Beamers.

He rang the doorbell at 821 (a yellow brick) and waited. Patches of grass were brown. Sod webworm, Funderburgh suspected. Too much watering at night. He had formulated prescriptions for the lawn's other deficiencies by the time he gave up and walked up the street toward the house at 825. Ah, well. Finn had warned him that the preponderance of two-income families in modern society (which Funderburgh deplored) would make it difficult for him to find neighbors at home during the day. But he wanted to get an early start.

Passing the Beamer house—red brick and green shutters—he couldn't help wondering: Did a murderess live there? If so, how had she killed her husband? Was she watching at this very moment from behind half-drawn blinds? These musings caused a shiver to pass through Funderburgh that was not entirely unpleasant. On impulse, he doubled back to the Beamer house and rang the doorbell without having any idea what he would say to the woman if she opened the door. But she didn't, even though Funderburgh rang again before he continued up the street. (The postman always rings twice, according to James M. Cain.)

The house at 825 was a radical departure in local architecture—a one-floor plan. Funderburgh rang the doorbell and contemplated the crab grass in the front yard. After a second ring and a one-minute wait, he headed back down the front walkway. But his departure was halted by the sound of the front door opening behind him.

A huge man stood in the doorway, which was narrower than he was. Funderburgh judged his height to be close to six feet and his weight as much as four hundred pounds. His arms were the size of thighs. He didn't have a neck and his head was a volley ball with hair. He carried a Diet Coke in one hand and a remote control device in the other.

"Can I help you?" the man wheezed. Each word was forced out of his lips under protest. Emphysema, Funderburgh diagnosed.

"I'm trying to find an old friend, but I seem to have the wrong address," Funderburgh said. The ease with which he lied filled him with both pride and shame. "His name is Otto Beamer. I haven't seen him in years."

"Maybe you better come in, sit down. I gotta sit down myself."

I have encountered the ultimate couch potato, Funderburgh thought. *He's shaped like a potato and big as a couch.*

"I don't want to take up your time."

"I wish you would."

Inside was like an ice house. Funderburgh shivered and regretted his short sleeves. His host, breathing heavily, led him down a narrow hallway to a family room. On one wall a twenty-four-inch TV screen was showing Michael Keaton as *Batman*, which

Funderburgh had enjoyed at the dollar movie one summer. Behind the TV was a brick wall lined with narrow shelves, and on the shelves were rows of video cassettes. Hundreds of them. Maybe a thousand.

The man switched off the movie, set down the remote control device, and stuck out his immense flipper of a hand. "Name's Hackleshin, Gus Hackleshin."

Funderburgh shook the sweaty hand and introduced himself. They sat down on opposite ends of a Naugahyde couch despite Funderburgh's fear that he would be propelled skyward by Hackleshin's weight, like a child on a teeter totter.

"Hate to break this to you, pal," Hackleshin said, "but your friend Otto bought the farm."

Funderburgh pretended puzzlement. "I didn't know Otto was interested in agriculture."

"I mean he's dead. You know, D-E-A-D, dead? Assumed room temperature. I hear the old ticker got him."

"Good heavens," Funderburgh said. "This is quite a shock."

"Guess he didn't suffer, if it makes you feel any better. That's the way to go, huh?" Hackleshin gulped down the remainder of his Diet Coke. "Get you a drink?"

Funderburgh declined. Here came the tricky part. "I know that Otto remarried. Did he and his wife get along? I'd like to think that Otto was happy in his final months."

Hackleshin shrugged his massive shoulders. "Couldn't say. I'm around every day, disability pension, but I'm pretty much stuck inside."

Having lived in a bachelor's residence all his adult life, Nelson Funderburgh knew from the ruffles on the couch and the cross stitching on the pillows that he was not in one now.

"Perhaps your wife could set my mind at ease?"

"Doubt it. She won't be home till kinda late anyway. Teaching her aerobics class after work. If you want the real skinny, pal, you oughta talk to the old lady across the street. She sees every damn thing. But, hey, wanna watch *Columbo*?"

Using all of his considerable diplomatic skills, Funderburgh eventually extricated himself from Otto Beamer's wheezing neighbor.

He had barely stepped onto the other side of the street when a black dog appeared at his side, barking furiously. Funderburgh had almost five decades of professional experience in dealing with dogs as a letter carrier, and by and large he liked them. This one was a Rottweiler—one of his favorite breeds.

"Snake! You leave that man alone!"

The apparent owner, bearing down on the animal with a dog chain and a terrifying look of determination, was a woman perhaps a couple of years older than Funderburgh and far more wrinkled. Her gray hair was in curlers and she was dressed in cutoff jeans topped by a checked shirt with the sleeves rolled up over withered arms.

"I wasn't frightened," Funderburgh told her.

"You should have been, mister. He bites."

She put the chain on the dog and tugged in the direction from which she had come.

"Just a minute," Funderburgh called. "Might I have a word with you, ma'am?"

Without halting, she turned her head in his direction to ask, "What're you selling?"

"Nothing, I assure you."

Stepping along with the woman, he told her of the distressing news he just received about Otto Beamer's sudden death. This time, seeing a more natural excuse to ask the kind of questions he wanted to ask, he presented himself as brother of the first Mrs. Beamer, who was eager to learn more about this second marriage.

"I know plenty." The woman paused on her front walk. "But I have to fix lunch for my son. Moved back home after his divorce, the big baby."

"I could help you cook."

She eyed Funderburgh with scorn. "A man?"

He drew himself up. Fighting words. "I have been cooking my own meals since I was eighteen, and I happen to be good at it."

"I doubt that. And how do I know you're not some kind of kinky sex-fiend killer just trying to get into my house?"

Funderburgh repressed a shudder. "I wouldn't worry if I were you. I mean, not with Snake around."

* * * * *

While dicing onions and celery for a luncheon omelet in the kitchen, Funderburgh learned that the tough-talking woman—Bessie Longdale—was a widow. So many women around his age were, he reflected in sadness. He'd met perhaps half a dozen lately, including that rather intriguing Mrs. Pertwee at the Famous Detectives School. Were their husbands' deaths a function of being male, truly the weaker sex, or did it have something to do with being married to these particular women? Certainly the latter was suspected in the case of the fiftyish Mrs. Beamer's spouse. But was it really so fishy that a seventy-four-year-old had died without warning? So many did. Funderburgh, feeling the weight of his years and a growing doubt about his mission, nevertheless pressed on.

"It would be nice to think that poor Otto was happy in his last months," he said, wiping back a timely but onion-induced tear with the hem of the gingham-checked apron she had insisted he wear.

Bessie Longdale snorted. "I don't doubt it. Never did see a woman carry on so over a man."

"His wife was attentive, then?"

"Attentive? That doesn't begin to tell it, mister. It was sickening. When they cooked out, she wouldn't even let him get his own beer."

Viola Beamer had scarcely acted like a murderess, then. But what Black Widow in her right mind *would*? And her excessive hovering over her husband, as observed by Mrs. Longdale, could be an indication of undue influence in the matter of the will. That reminded Funderburgh of the competency question.

"Was Otto sharp until the end?"

"He married a younger babe who runs around with her tummy showing and got her to wait on him hand and foot, didn't he?" Mrs. Longdale slipped the Rottweiler a piece of sausage. "Wish I was sharp enough to cut a deal like that."

Funderburgh didn't like the speculative gaze she leveled at him. He had perhaps displayed too much eagerness and aptitude in the culinary line. And his lack of progeny would be a plus on several fronts for a matrimonially inclined widow. He put down the paring knife and took off the apron while continuing to talk.

"Did they have many friends, visitors?" He almost said "witnesses."

Mrs. Longdale shook her curler-laden head. "They pretty much kept to themselves. If she said 'hi' it was a lot. His son used to come around once in a while, but I haven't seen him for ages. Her son came, too, but only when Otto was gone to his VFW meeting. I don't think those two got along."

"How did you know he was Mrs. Beamer's son?"

"She introduced us. Snake almost bit him once when he was coming out of her house. Not my type. He looked like one of those guys on the cough drop box—you know, the Smith Brothers?"

* * * * *

From behind the blinds across the street, Viola Beamer watched the elderly man leave Bessie Longdale's house. He'd been with the old gossip half an hour, and with that slob up the street before that. She was sure that he was the one who rang her doorbell while she was showering, though he was already outside the Hackleshin house by the time she made it to the door. Couldn't be a Jehovah's Witness; they always hunted in pairs. And he wasn't carrying anything to sell. So what was his game?

Strangers in the neighborhood bothered her. For years she'd had this creepy fantasy that someday a man she didn't know, a cop or insurance investigator, would ring her doorbell and it would all be over.

But that wasn't going to happen, not ever. She was too smart to get caught, too smart to leave traces—or to attract attention. With her money she could have begun living like a queen a long time ago. But she'd kept her third-shift job and her middle-class lifestyle. That's why nobody ever gave her so much as a suspicious look when she put out her hand to collect the life insurance settlements and the inheritances.

When the latest haul was paid and invested with the rest she'd have nine hundred and twenty-five thousand dollars salted away in stocks, bonds, and treasury bills. Just another seventy-five thousand and she'd have her million dollars—all she ever wanted. She didn't even have to marry another old goat to get it. All she had to do was die. Then she would be born again. New name, new lifestyle. Subconsciously she fingered the pendant around her neck as she imagined how she would spend the money. Clothes. Cars. Jewels.

But she wouldn't show off and she wouldn't get greedy. Greed was where most murderers made their mistake. A million was enough for her. It was more than anybody else ever dreamed of when she was a kid in Casey County with clothes always out of style and a mother who cleaned bed pans to scratch out a living. She'd earned it, though. The things she'd done...

Viola Beamer shook off the memories as she watched the stranger in the neighborhood slide into a blue Dodge Colt and drive away.

FIVE

WEDDING BELLS AND DEATH KNELLS

Rosalee Chandler liked striding down the wide hallways of the Hamilton County Court House, her heels clicking on the marble floors. It wasn't as modern or as well-lit as the library where she worked, but it was awesome.

At least the recently refurbished hallways were. The offices themselves, with their black and green linoleum floors and dirty white walls, always depressed Chandler. She'd spent a lot of time in these dingy rooms researching unsuspecting citizens since she'd joined the Famous Detectives School. It was her sleuthing specialty.

Before coming to the Court House today, she'd already learned Viola Beamer's birth date (56 years ago) and home town (Casey County, Kentucky) from county voter registration records, as well as the irrelevant fact that she was a Democrat. Using the birth date, Chandler was able to get a former boyfriend at the Ohio Bureau of Motor Vehicles to give her all the data from Viola's driver's license, including height, weight, social security number and, of course, license number. She also found that Viola was supposed to wear glasses for driving and that she'd had two speeding citations and four parking tickets.

Court records could yield a further gold mine of information if Mrs. Beamer had ever been involved in either civil or criminal court action. But to make a complete search of the subject, down to her school and work history, Chandler would have to know Viola Beamer's maiden name. She could get that by looking up the woman's marriage license on the fifth floor of the Court House. She bounded up the steps.

Everybody at the Famous Detectives School, including Mr. Finn, thought Chandler had joined the school only because she wanted to improve her research skills in order to be a better librarian. But that was just a front. The real reason, which she'd told nobody in this world, was to learn the special skills needed to trace her biological father.

For most of her twenty-four years the identity of the two unmarried teenagers who had given her life was of little interest to Chandler. Her real parents were the couple who had diapered her, seen her through the crushing disappointments of adolescence, and helped her pay her way through college. But less than a year ago, she'd received word from a state agency that her birth mother was in need of a kidney transplant from a compatible donor. Would she be willing? She had agreed without hesitation. There was a tearful meeting, an all-too-short time of getting to know each other, then a parting without a goodbye. Chandler's kidney tissue proved incompatible after all, and her birth mother died before a suitable donor could be found.

With her mother found and then lost again, Chandler began wondering for the first time about her father. Her mother hadn't been sure how to spell his last name. She remembered the general area where he'd lived more than two decades ago in Covington, Kentucky, just across the Ohio River, though not the particular street. And she could recall the name of a buddy with whom he'd hung around.

That should be enough for Chandler to find her father, using the interviewing skills and advanced paper-trail techniques that she had now learned at the Famous Detectives School. But did she really want to? According to her mother, he didn't even know about her. Would it be fair to burst into his life at this point? He could be a family man with a wife and other children. Even so, maybe he would be happy to learn about her; maybe he would love her. But did she want to get to know the man, then lose him, too, someday down the road?

She'd made a preliminary foray once into her father's old neighborhood—but half-heartedly, racked by indecision about whether to proceed. In the end she'd held off. Impersonal names on paper records or on a computer screen, people she'd never met and never would, were always a lot easier for Chandler to deal with than real human beings. Especially men.

For weeks now, the only man in her life had been Francis Aloysius Finn. He wasn't at all what she'd expected of a private detective. He was short, about forty pounds overweight, and never tried to be a tough guy, like that obnoxious Joe Canova. But Chandler had learned from experience that his lectures were sound. Mr. Finn knew everything about detective work—except how to make money at it, judging from his school's Early Goodwill decor.

So here she was, doing another homework assignment for him. She never minded giving up her lunch hour for Famous Detectives School business because she never had other plans.

In room 536 of the Hamilton County Court House, Chandler seated herself in a straight-backed chair in front of three NCR computer units spread out on two long tables pushed together. When one of the green screens gave her five options of types of records she could look at, she selected the marriage license index. A screen came up with four columns: LAST NAME, GIVEN NAME, SPOUSE FULL NAME, LIC. NO. Scrolling down the B's under LAST NAME, Chandler found Beamer, Otto, Viola Rosselli, and the license number. If the license had been issued this year, she could have given the number to the blue-haired clerk with magenta glasses and gotten an immediate look at the license itself. But because it had been issued last year, it was now on microfilm. Chandler went across the hall to room 537 to look it up.

She made a copy of the license just in case, but there appeared to be nothing surprising about it. Both spouses' names, ages, residences, states of birth, occupations, parents' names and previous marriages were listed, along with a signed statement at the bottom that the Rev. Mason Eaton had performed the wedding ceremony on the 24th of December the year before. Each spouse claimed one previous marriage, ending in death of the spouse's original partner. Had there been a divorce, the case number and court would have been given, which could have yielded all sorts of juicy details.

Viola's father's surname was given as Hackett. Presumably, then, that was her maiden name. Any records of her in the court system could be under Hackett, Rosselli, or Beamer. Chandler could have stopped there. But her own instincts as a researcher, reinforced by Finn's anecdote-laden lecture on the paper trail, impelled her onward. She looked up Victor Rosselli, Viola's previous husband, in the marriage license index. There were two licenses on file—one for a marriage to Guilia Martini in 1947 and another for a marriage to Viola Van Wert in 1987. Chandler stared at the name "Van Wert." She had been expecting to see "Hackett" as Viola's pre-marriage name.

Mystified by the discrepancy, she pulled up the license itself on microfilm. It was the same Viola, all right. The parents' names were identical with those on the license of marriage to Otto Beamer. But this document indicated one previous marriage—to Richard Van Wert, deceased.

Goose bumps marched up Chandler's back and arms. Something weird was going on here. Viola had been widowed *twice* before she married Otto Beamer, not just once. And by listing only one previous marriage on her most recent marriage license application, Viola Hackett Rosselli Beamer had opened herself to a charge of marriage license falsification.

At the least.

Chandler went back to the computer in room 536 to look up the marriage of Richard Van Wert and Viola—Somebody.

SIX

TRASH, MAN

Even the sound of good jazz pouring out of the Chevy S10 pickup's radio did nothing to improve the mood of the driver.

Oh, man, thought Shadd Davis, *why did I have to get stuck with this trash gig?*

There was only one logical explanation: prejudice. Mr. Finn must have some funky prejudice against musicians. He'd been playing his sax on the sidewalk for two years, ever since the GM plant closed.

Stealing garbage wasn't anywhere near what Davis had in mind when he'd decided to become a private eye. He wanted to take out the bad guys, especially the pushers. Put 'em away for good. Take back his neighborhood from the drug lords, make it safe for his little brothers and sisters. Bad Shadd, Scourge of Evil Doers. *That's* why he'd responded to that ad he saw on a matchbook cover: "Do you have what it takes to be a **PRIVATE EYE**?" Maybe he should have joined the FBI instead. But the FBI wasn't into dreadlocks and earrings. Davis wanted to be able to express his individuality and still catch crooks. Like Batman.

Yeah, right. So here he was prowling this lily-white neighborhood behind the wheel of his brother's truck. Mission: garbage. This was worse than a two-day gig in Gary, Indiana. Shaft wouldn't be caught dead doing this.

Got to be incon*spic*uous, Mr. Finn had said. Don't want to attract attention stealing trash, even though the Supreme Court said it wasn't stealing at all. *So what I have to do,* Davis thought, *is to take trash bags from all over the street, not just the ones Mr. Finn really wants. Anybody sees me, they just think I'm a scavenger, not a sly private eye checking out the Beamers' trash.* Scavengers came into neighborhoods like this to pick out the good stuff every garbage day, according to Mr. Finn.

And garbage day happened to be Friday, just two days after he pulled this cool assignment. What luck.

Davis pulled onto Cherry Tree Lane and parked his brother's truck in front of the first house on the same side of the street as the Beamer residence. Or rather, he parked in front of its garbage, stacked neatly on the strip of grass between the street and the sidewalk. He opened the truck's glove compartment and pulled out a pair of heavy work gloves he'd bought at Walmart after Wednesday's class. He got out of the truck, lifted the tops off the four trash cans, and tossed the plastic garbage bags he found inside into the back of the truck.

That wasn't so bad after all. The folks who lived in this house probably had a garbage disposer, so there weren't any half-eaten oranges or rotten apples in the bag. Still, he was glad he hadn't eaten breakfast. There was a distinct whiff of disposable diaper coming from the third bag.

Davis eased the truck down to the next house and did it again. He was faster the second time around.

In two more stops he was in front of the Beamer house. There wasn't much to set it apart from any of the other houses on the street except the number. Red brick, like half the others, aluminum siding, like all the others. No individuality. Davis shook his dreadlocks in disgust as he removed the Beamer trash, only two cans. He stacked the bags from those cans to one side in the truck, so they'd stand out later when he was ready go through them for clues.

Clues—now you're talking, Davis thought.

With the Beamer trash safely on board, he kept going down the street. Two more houses ought to be enough to make it look good to any nosy folks peeking out their windows this morning. Then he could get the hell out of here, take Mr. Finn the garbage he wanted to see, and get rid of the rest. Davis hadn't figured out the getting-rid-of part yet, but he'd think of something.

He was pulling in front of the last house when he saw the flashing light of a police cruiser in his rear vision mirror.

Oh, *man*. Davis put on the brakes and turned off the ignition.

Incon*spic*uous, he thought. Yeah, right.

The officer parked behind the truck and walked over to the driver's side window. He was about as fair as Davis was black, maybe five years younger than Davis's twenty-eight, and—unlike a lot of older cops—hadn't yet had to punch extra holes in his belt.

He bent his head down to the level of Davis's window. "May I please see your driver's license, sir?"

"No problemo," Davis said. He pulled the license out of his wallet and handed it over. "I don't mind. I've got nothin' to hide. In fact, I've got a Constitutional *right* to take that garbage. The Supreme Court said so, May 16, 1988." He remembered the date from Mr. Finn's lecture because May 16 was his mother's birthday and 88 was the number of keys on a piano.

"That may be, sir," the officer said, "but your license plates are expired."

Damn! That lazy shit-for-brains brother of his hadn't bothered to get new plates. That never happened to Shaft. Davis sunk into his seat, boiling mad.

The policeman, using a walkie-talkie on his shoulder, radioed in the data off of Davis's license. Davis waited for a squawked reply before he said, "Look, officer, this ain't even my pickup."

"I know that."

"It belongs to my brother, see—"

"The last name on the registration for this vehicle is Douglas, sir, not Davis."

"I mean half-brother."

Davis could hear his own voice getting shrill. These explanations were a pain in the ass. He wanted to get on with his assignment, the trash sitting in the back of the truck.

The officer stepped away and talked into his gizmo again before he came back to Davis.

"Sir, we're going to have to go to the township police station to get this straightened out. We can call your brother from there and I'm sure everything will be okay. You drive the truck and I'll follow you. Please drive slowly. Do you know where the station is?"

Davis didn't, not being well-acquainted with this suburban part of town, but the policeman gave him instructions. Two steep hills and one sharp turn later he pulled into the station with the officer behind. From a phone inside they woke up Mel Douglas and got his ass to the station to identify Davis and take the ticket for the expired license plate. When the time came to pay up, Mel pulled a plastic card out of his wallet.

"Sorry, sir," the officer told him. "We can't accept American Express."

"Shit, man." He looked at Davis. "You got the ducats, bro?"

By the time Davis left the station, screaming at his tree-sized half-brother as they went through the door, it was past noon. Davis went right to the back of the truck, fearful about the contents of trash bags sitting in the sun all those hours.

What he found was even worse than he'd imagined. That sharp left turn and the dips on the way to the station had thrown the trash bags together like a bunch of unemployed saxophonists sleeping at a homeless shelter. No longer were the all-important Beamer bags set off to the right. They were mixed in somewhere amidst the everyday worthless trash bags, about a dozen of them in all, mostly the same black color.

"What the matter, man?" Mel asked. "You look pale."

"I just wasted the whole frigging morning, that's all, shithead."

With the bags lumped all together like that, Davis had no idea which were the ones Mr. Finn wanted him to get and which were just—trash.

SEVEN

DEATH NOTICES

Francis Aloysius Finn was not a superstitious man. Still, he was strongly tempted to blame Joe Canova's appearance in his office on the date: Friday, July the 13th.

The unpromising student barged in, breathless with excitement, as Finn was dictating lecture notes to Hilary Kendrake—notes that would put him a few days ahead of schedule for the first time in weeks.

"I got him." Canova waved a videotape in his right hand. "I nailed the bastard!"

The fireman-writer-sleuth could only be referring to John Adams, the subject in the insurance case Canova had been fumbling with since June. He once lost the subject on a simple stakeout assignment because he, Canova, ducked into McDonald's to use the bathroom. That had been before the wide-mouth-jar lecture, of course.

"High time," Finn said. "And which particular ploy ensnared the miscreant?"

"It was simple as a self-winding watch," Canova said, his lustful eyes darting toward the attractive Kendrake as he talked. "I let the air out of one of his back tires, then sit myself on a bus stop bench across the street and videotape what happens. He gets in the car and drives about two feet when he catches on that a tire's going *kerplopp, kerplopp*. So he gets out, throws his cane on the ground and jacks up the car to change the tire. So much for lower back pain." Canova waved the videotape again. "I got it all right here. How about a look-see, Finn?"

"The customary written report would be sufficient for our purposes. The insurance company will, of course, be thrilled to see the tape as documentation."

"But I want to show it to you," Canova pressed. "It's a scream."

On second thought, Finn reflected, it wouldn't be a bad idea to preview the tape before he sent it on to Cheviot Mutual. How else could he be certain that Canova hadn't put his hand over the camera or erased the tape?

"Unfortunately," Finn said, "we don't have a VCR here in the office."

"The Blockbuster Video next door rents them," Kendrake said. "I could go get one and you could charge it to Cheviot Mutual on your expense account."

The Compleat Secretary. What a gem! "That's an excellent idea, Mrs. Kendrake. Please do." Kendrake departed, leaving Finn to suffer fifteen excruciating minutes with Canova before she returned with the VCR and a 20-inch television.

The three of them cleared off a small table in Finn's office and sat back to watch.

On the tape, a man who was presumably John Adams walked out of a sad-looking apartment house leaning on an aluminum cane. He got behind the wheel of an ancient green Buick Riviera and, as Canova reported, drove only a few feet before halting. When Adams confirmed the flat tire by visual inspection, he flew into a rage and hurled his cane to the sidewalk. At that moment, his flushed face was almost directly in line with the camera.

"Hold it!" Finn cried. "Hold that picture."

Kendrake, who held the remote control, hit the "pause" button. The cane-thrower's face froze on the screen. Sagging jowls and mournful eyes gave him the countenance of an unhappy bulldog. Finn shoved his own visage within five inches of the TV.

"I know that reprobate!" he announced after a moment's study confirmed his suspicion. "His name isn't Adams. It's Hawley Smoot."

"You sure?"

"Positive, Mr. Canova. I had the distinct displeasure of getting up-close and personal with Smoot several times when I worked for the prosecuting attorney's office. He's developed a paunch and taken to wearing an ill-fitting wig apparently made of Chihuahua hair, but I'm certain it's the same pathetic individual."

"Are we talking major criminal here?" Kendrake asked.

"No, we are talking sleazebag-at-large. I mean small-time burglary, pickpocketing, con games that prey on the elderly. And that's just for financial gain. What he does for amusement is even worse. One time he was caught trying to suck a lady's toes in the public library. Insurance fraud is a new one for him, though. I'm going to enjoy nipping that in the bud. Good work, indeed, Mr. Canova. I'm proud of you." In high good humor, Finn didn't even add "at last."

"I knew I'd get him," Canova smirked. "I just had a few setbacks along the way."

"How soon can you get me the written report?"

Canova, perennially late with his over-written reports, was spared having to answer by the sound of the bell signaling the opening of the front door in the outer office.

"I'll get it," Kendrake said, handing Finn the remote as she left the room.

"Finish the tape," Canova urged.

Taxing his mechanical aptitude to its limits, Finn managed to push the proper button to take the machine out of its "pause" mode. The rest of the tape was as damning as Canova had promised. No one with the permanent lower-back disability being claimed by Adams/Smoot could have changed a tire as he did.

Finn was rewinding the tape with a smile on his face when Kendrake returned with Rosalee Chandler, who was dressed in a short-sleeved yellow dress that cried summer.

"I've got the goods on Viola Beamer." Chandler brandished her loose-leaf notebook and a manila folder.

Something in the bounce of Chandler's auburn hair always made Finn mourn his lost youth. She was a striking girl, and he couldn't blame Canova for preening in her presence. She made Finn feel fatherly and protective, certainly not romantic. Finn preferred the company of women with ripe beauty and mature grace—like Mrs. Kendrake, for example. A highly hypothetical example, of course. What was that song from *The Music Man*—"A Sadder but Wiser Girl for Me," wasn't it?

Finn regarded Chandler as his greatest achievement in the Famous Detectives School, however. Applying herself with a seriousness that Finn feared was almost unhealthy at her age, she mastered every research skill he taught her. Whatever she had on Viola would be worthwhile.

"Let's hear it." Finn tossed the remote onto his desk and banished Hawley Smoot from his mind.

While Kendrake sat down, Chandler opened the notebook. "Viola Beamer is a Democrat, votes regularly. She drives a four-year-old Escort, Ohio license plate VH-499. Two traffic tickets to her name, not counting parking violations. Payments are current on all four of her charge cards."

A model citizen, Finn thought.

"She was born fifty-six years ago in Casey County, Kentucky. One of five kids. Father died before Viola was born, leaving her mother impoverished. Viola dropped out of high school at age sixteen and married a local boy with prospects. He was a builder. They moved to Cincinnati. After twenty-one years he abandoned her and started over with another sixteen-year-old."

"Likes 'em young," Canova said with a leer at Chandler.

"Apparently he did all right for himself financially," Chandler went on, ignoring Canova, "but Viola never saw any of it. That same year he left her she was arrested for shoplifting two cans of Spaghettios. Court records show her repeated attempts to collect alimony. No child support—no record of kids. Viola worked at various menial jobs until eleven years ago, when she took a position with the Fairlawn Nursing Home as a Licensed Practical Nurse. The Ohio Board of Nursing says she isn't one, though. She's worked at a number of other nursing homes since, but Fairlawn is the one where she met her second husband. He was seventy-six years old and died seven months after they married."

"Interesting," Finn murmured.

"I haven't even gotten to the interesting part yet. Take a look at this."

She handed Finn the manila file folder, stuffed with paperwork. He opened it and found on top a copy of a newspaper's obituary page. One of the death notices was circled in red:

VAN WERT
Richard G., beloved husband of Viola (née Graf), devoted father of Wanda James, Albany, N.Y., and Leonard Van Wert of Hong Kong,

dear grandfather of Susan and Jennifer Van Wert. Tuesday, April 9. Age 71. Mr. Van Wert worked for the U.S. Postal Service for 37 years. He was Secretary of the Letter Carriers Association and was a Deacon and Trustee of the Far Hills Community Presbyterian Church. Friends may call 2-5 P.M. Sunday at the Eternal Rest Funeral Home, 1135 Schaefer Pike. Funeral service 10 A.M. Tuesday, April 14.

Finn looked up to find Chandler watching him.

"'Beloved husband of Viola,'" he quoted.

Chandler nodded and Finn frowned. "I thought her married name before Beamer was Rosselli," he said.

"It was," Chandler said. "Husband Van Wert predated Rosselli." She plucked a wad of microfilm prints out of the folder. "And before him came Graf, and before Graf came Hunnicut, and before Hunnicut came Squires. The woman was married six times, counting Beamer and the one who left her, and widowed five."

"Hell of a habit," Canova commented.

"This is dynamite," Finn told her. "How did you get on to it?"

"I just kept tracing back the marriage licenses until they dead-ended at her maiden name forty years ago in Kentucky," Chandler said. "The last five husbands were all within the past eleven years—and all elderly men whose children, if any, mostly lived out of town. Beamer was an exception on that score."

"But Norris and his father had been estranged for some time," Finn pointed out.

"So the son was no threat to her," Chandler said. "Another thing in common among the last five is that they were all government employees of some kind."

Finn nodded. "Famously generous pensions, which means they could all afford sizeable insurance policies and probably left behind tidy inheritances. None of them by himself would be rich enough to draw a lot of unhealthy attention to the widow, but it added up nicely."

"Sounds suspicious to me," Canova said.

Finn glared. *There has to be one in every class.*

"It's hard to imagine a woman could just kill five husbands without somebody noticing," Kendrake said with a shiver.

"Imagination is not required," Finn said. "There was once a school bus driver near Schenectady who buried all nine of her children over ten years. Eventually she was convicted of one killing and admitted to at least three others. A succession of husbands ought to be even easier to get away with: The woman changes her name when she marries, moves into the man's house, maybe gets a different job, adopts a whole new circle of friends who don't know about husbands one through five. It's been done."

"The four elderly husbands before Beamer were cremated," Chandler said. "Just like he was."

"How do you know that?" Canova asked.

"I checked the death certificates at the Health Department. Mr. Finn talked about that in the lecture week before last, remember?"

"Oh, yeah. Sure."

"No body, no evidence," Kendrake mused. "Proving murder 'beyond a reasonable doubt' would be quite a challenge."

"We'll have to collect circumstantial evidence." Finn looked at his two students. "Any suggestions?"

"Somebody ought to talk to the funeral director who handled Beamer," Chandler said. "Maybe Viola said or did something around him that will seem suspicious, knowing what we know."

"It's worth a shot." Finn meant exactly that and nothing more: Chances of success were not great, but it was something to do and it would provide useful experience for one of his sleuths. "You, Mr. Canova."

"What about me?"

"You wanted a piece of this case—now you have it. Talk to the funeral director."

Canova fumbled for a cigarette. "Talking to people isn't exactly my strong suit."

"Probably not," Finn said, "but you have to learn. The main thing to remember here is to be subtle with your questions. We don't want to get the word around that we're on to Mrs. Beamer."

Canova lit up and took a deep drag. "I don't think I have the time. I still have to write you a report to go with the videotape."

"Yes, but that won't take long."

From the manila folder, Finn pulled out the copy of Otto Beamer's death notice. He copied down the name and address of the funeral home on the back of an unpaid telephone bill for Canova's benefit.

"Listen, Finn," Canova said, "the bottom line is, I don't like funeral homes. They give me the creeps."

Chandler waved away cigarette smoke. "You mean you're afraid of dead bodies?"

"Hell, no." Canova flushed. "I just don't like 'em, is all."

"They won't hurt you."

"I know they— Oh, shit. If you're going to make a big deal out of it, I'll do it."

Finn handed him the funeral home's address.

Chandler glanced at her watch. "Oops, I'd better get to work. All the documentation for what I told you is in that folder."

"I'm sure it is," Finn said.

Canova and Chandler departed together, leaving Finn shaking his head.

"She can take care of herself," Kendrake said with a smile, breaking into his thoughts.

"I have no doubt about that." Finn rested his moon-shaped head on his hand. "I just hope she can take care of him."

"When you mentioned insurance before, that set me thinking. If Viola Beamer murdered Otto, doesn't that mean she couldn't be the beneficiary of his insurance? And wouldn't Norris get it as next of kin?"

"Yes! Absolutely!" Finn slapped his right hand on the desk. "Good thinking, Mrs. Kendrake! Those tightwads at Cheviot Mutual are going to hear about this."

Finn didn't much like Norris Beamer, but a client was a client and it was Finn's duty to protect his clients' interests. He grabbed the phone and punched in the number of his old friend Calvin Jefferson, Cheviot Mutual's chief investigator. Calvin farmed out most of the actual work, largely to Finn and other PIs, but he bore the ultimate responsibility.

"Calvin? Your instincts were right about that Adams claim," Finn said. "It was as spurious as the claimant's name and hairpiece, and I have a videotape to prove it."

"Yeah?" Calvin said in his rich baritone. "I love those funny home videos."

"This one is hilarious. And it stars an old acquaintance of mine."

After discussing the identity and history of the pseudonymous Adams, and promising a written report to follow, Finn changed the subject:

"Calvin, I have reason to believe that one of your beneficiaries hastened your client's departure from his vale of tears."

"We kind of frown on that," Calvin said.

Finn briefed the insurance investigator on the unseemly number of cremated husbands in Mrs. Beamer's past. Calvin promised to make some inter-office calls and get back to Finn pronto. Within ten minutes he called to report that, an elderly man's heart attack death being in no way unusual, Mrs. Beamer's claim was proceeding normally. The hundred-thousand-dollar death benefit had not yet been paid, however.

"Make sure that it isn't, Calvin," Finn pleaded. "Get your people to stall, lie, drag their feet, do whatever they have to do to hold off paying that claim for at least a few weeks. In other words, do what they always do, only more so."

"I think I can manage that." Finn could imagine Calvin twirling his horn-rimmed glasses. "Might save me some trouble later. The guy had no history of heart problems, right? That should do for an excuse to slow things up a bit."

"You're a gentleman and a scholar, Calvin."

Finn hung up the phone with a grin on his face.

"Who says Friday the 13th is unlucky?" he asked Kendrake.

"I think Viola Beamer would," she replied, "if she knew what we were up to today."

"Let's just hope that Canova doesn't blow his assignment."

"He really did seem quite reluctant, didn't he?"

EIGHT

MUMMY'S BOY

Joe Canova stubbed out a cigarette, the third since he'd been sitting in his Mustang outside the Colonial-style building on Schaefer Pike.

In his mind's ear he could hear the Spanish-accented voice of his ex-wife. "Smoking kills, Joe." At least he didn't have to listen to that crap anymore. He shut the voice out and pulled another Camel from the half-empty box.

Eternal Rest Funeral Home, the sign on the building said in fancy script that was supposed to look like handwriting. This was the establishment that had handled what was politely called the "arrangements" for Otto Beamer's body.

Canova hated funeral homes since, as an eight-year-old boy, he'd been forced to sit in front of his Aunt Dottie's stone-cold body for the entire visitation. How long did visitations last back then? In Canova's memories it seemed like days. He'd never seen a dead body before, never even known anyone who'd died. And she was his favorite aunt, the one who always listened to him. As she rested between satin sheets in the coffin, wearing a nightgown, Joey was sure she'd sit up any minute so he could tell her how much he hated the funeral parlor with its sickening-sweet smell of flowers and death. But she never did.

The grownup Joe Canova lit yet another cigarette, chasing away wisps of memory with clouds of smoke. He wasn't afraid of funeral homes, he reminded himself. He just hated them. They gave him the creeps. So did undertakers. Those people had to be a few bricks short of a load to stand being around dead people all the time. If they weren't nuts when they started, they damned sure were after they'd been at it a few years. Maybe they even liked their jobs, the way he liked putting out fires. Talk about sick.

Canova realized he was babbling in his mind, but he was sure he wasn't stalling. If he wanted to stall he could write up his report on that asshole with the phony insurance claim. That's what Finn told him to do. Canova didn't like being told what to do. He'd get to the paperwork in his own sweet time, probably on his next day off. He was a writer, wasn't he? But he was also a man of action— fire fighter, private eye, lover.

Alina probably thought he'd be pining away for her ever since she filed the divorce papers on him without warning. Ha. Not him. Canova realized now she only married him so she could stay in this country. She never believed in him, or his writing. So the hell with her. He was in the market for new female companionship.

Like maybe Rosalee Chandler, Canova thought as he sucked deeply on his cigarette. She was prettier than Alina, and better built. And she made that Mary Sue Barkeloo with her bubble gum seem like a kid by comparison. His one date with Barkeloo ended quickly and badly. Canova could practically feel her slap in his face whenever he looked at her. And he looked at her a lot. But he was sure Chandler would be more receptive to him once he put on the full court press. *She comes across so cool and all-business, but I'll melt her down.*

Too bad she hadn't been around when Canova showed Finn his own version of "Candid Camera," starring Hawley Smoot, a.k.a. John Adams. She would have been impressed by the way he cracked that case. But this Viola Beamer deal was bigger. Murder One, it looked like, from what Chandler herself had dug up. So she'd be even more impressed if he came back from the Eternal Rest Funeral Home with something to clinch the case.

Oh, all right. Canova got out of the Mustang, flattened his cigarette on the pavement with a shoe, and walked past the phony porch columns into the funeral home without pausing.

Inside the door was a wide hallway with two arched doorways on the right. In front of each stood a black sign with white stick-on letters identifying the deceased individual on view inside, or soon to be. Canova took in the setup at a glance, then ducked through a doorway on his left.

As he'd expected, the room was an office. A woman with hair the color of a mouse and teeth like a rabbit sat at a green metal desk, typing into a computer terminal. On one corner of the desk, next to a phone console loaded with buttons, rested a glass vase with three or four yellow flowers. It could have been the office of a trucking company or a Realtor. But to Canova it smelled of death. His nose was full of the stench, crammed with it. He wanted to stop breathing.

"Excuse me," he said to the woman at the desk, "I'd like to see the manager."

"Oh!" She looked up from the computer, startled. "Sorry, I didn't see you." She stretched her lips into a smile, reshaping her angular face and knocking ten years off Canova's estimate of her age. Make it fifty now.

"The manager," Canova repeated.

"That would be the director, Mr. Greylock. I'm sorry, but he's with a bereaved family right now."

"I'll wait."

"Do you have an appointment?" The tone of her voice told Canova she knew he didn't.

"Just give him this."

Canova handed over one of his business cards. He had a dozen or more, describing him variously as a reporter, photographer, collector, electrician, insurance agent, and so on. He had never actually used any of them, not even this one. It said:

JOSEPH CANOVA
Investigator

It didn't say licensed, because he wasn't. And it didn't say *A-Plus Detective Agency* because Finn would have shit fits if Canova started throwing that name around. Before long Canova would take a hike from Finn's chicken outfit, but not until he'd sucked up the savvy and the contacts he needed. He'd only signed up for the class to learn about private eyes for his writing, but now he saw that he could make some decent dough as a PI during his off days from the fire house.

While the secretary glanced at the card, Canova settled in a plush chair facing the desk. She flashed him an irritated look and disappeared into an adjoining room.

Left behind, Canova wished he'd spent the half hour in his car figuring out how he was going to approach this interview.

Some story about being a friend of the Beamer family, maybe? It would be damned hard to get from there to, "Did this babe look like a killer to you?" Maybe he would have to play it straight. Finn wanted him to be subtle, but where did subtle ever get anybody? Mike Hammer was about as subtle as a train wreck and he always got the crook *and* the girl.

Canova looked around him. Odd to think that beyond these walls, in the same building, were those stiffs lying cold, not breathing…

The rabbit-toothed woman, now wearing an expression that could have been induced by sucking on a persimmon, returned from the other office and shut the door behind her.

"Mr. Greylock will see you as soon as he's free."

Canova nodded and followed the woman with his eyes as she sat down. The nameplate on the top of her desk said "Maisie Wandstradt." She was wearing a blue paisley dress that looked as if it had been swiped from a corpse getting the cheapest funeral offered by the Eternal Rest Funeral Home.

"Nice outfit, Maisie," Canova said.

She typed on in stony silence.

Next to her nameplate was a red-on-white plastic sign warning **NO SMOKING**.

"Mind if I smoke?" Canova asked. The smell would blot out the odor of death.

Maisie Wandstradt stopped typing and looked at him. "Smoking is bad for you, Mr. Canova."

"So I hear."

"A lot of our clients were smokers. We have several convenient payment options if you'd like to pre-plan your funeral." The secretary managed a tight smile. "Would you care to look at a brochure?"

"Do you have anything else to read?"

Before she could respond, the door from the other office opened. Out stepped a man about an inch taller than Canova, with brown hair a few shades lighter than Canova's dark locks. The hair was waved, combed back, and ragged at the fringes of his neck. A neatly trimmed beard covered most of his thin face, but what wasn't covered was pale. He wore a six-hundred-dollar blue suit, the same shade as his eyes, with a white carnation in the lapel.

Canova was glad that on the way over he'd stopped to clip on a tie and squeeze himself into the only sport jacket he owned.

"Mr. Canova?" He mispronounced it *Canova*. "I'm Samuel Greylock. The funeral director."

He put his hand out. Canova rose and shook it. He figured Greylock's age at nearing forty, which put him at the other end the thirties from Canova.

"How can I help you?" Greylock asked with a practiced smile. He held Canova's card in his left hand.

Oily bastard, Canova thought. "It's a private matter."

"Then let's discuss it privately." Greylock waved Canova into the room behind him with a sweep of his hand. "Have a seat and I'll be with you in a moment."

Inside Greylock's office, a mahogany desk the size of an aircraft carrier was positioned in front of a set of closed French doors. The two doors held stained glass windows forming a single image of Jesus rising from the dead, leaving the empty burial cave behind. The bereaved family Greylock had been with must have gone out those doors.

Canova sat in an ornate wooden chair with a well-upholstered seat. His feet rested on hardwood flooring, exposed except where it was covered by an oriental rug that must have been worth approximately half the national debt—if it wasn't fake.

Around the room were placed pieces of antique furniture whose names and even functions were beyond him. Then over in the corner was an object that looked like a *papier-mâché* Great Dane covered in gold paint. But that would have been so out of sync with the decor that Canova figured it must be something else. Victorian art, maybe.

Greylock re-entered the room and slipped behind the desk to sit in an overstuffed chair with a high back. "Now," he said with the same prefabricated grin showing through his beard, "what's this about? Your card says you're an investigator. What do you investigate?"

"Right now, I'm looking into some potential irregularities involving one of your st— uh, clients." Put him on the defense, make him eager to show his innocence by helping.

"What kind of irregularities?" Greylock sat forward, both hands on the desk. "Which client?"

"It's nothing you did wrong," Canova assured him. Now he'd be relieved, co-operative. "You understand, from this point on, anything I tell you must be in the strictest confidence."

"Discretion is my professional watchword. Please continue."

"Right. First let me tell you that I can't mention my client's name."

"I understand. Client confidentiality."

Canova nodded and pulled a notebook out of his inside pocket. "This confidential client of mine has reason to think there might be something fishy about his father's death—a man you laid out here, name of Otto Beamer."

"Beamer?" For a moment the bearded mortician seemed lost in thought. "Oh, yes. The retired IRS employee earlier this month. But he was an old man!"

"His wife was younger." Canova searched the desk top with his eyes. Just as he thought—not an ash tray in sight. "It's the wife I want to ask you about. Did you ever see her before she came to you for his funeral?"

"No." Smile. "But that isn't unusual. Many families have been with us for generations, of course, but our high standard of service also wins many referrals. New business is always welcome."

"I'll keep that in mind. How did Mrs. Beamer act when you saw her? Was she nervous, upset—guilty-acting?"

"I tend to think that all mourners feel a little guilty." Greylock sat back with a self-satisfied expression as he made a tepee of his fingers. "After all, they're alive and the loved one isn't. And then they think of things they should have done for Uncle Fred or said to Mom but never did. I've been in this industry seventeen years, Mr. Canova"—*Canova*—"including twelve years as the director here, and I would say that Mrs. Beamer behaved much as I would expect any widow to behave."

"Practice," Canova grunted to himself as he wrote in his notebook.

"What's that?"

"The name's Can*o*va."

"Oh, sorry."

"But about Mrs. Beamer?"

"She seemed like a pleasant-enough woman. That's about all I can add. May I ask what brought about these suspicions of foul play?"

"The four previous husbands, all of them elderly, all of them dead, seemed a bit much," Canova confided. "So did the fact that all of them were cremated, conveniently making it impossible to dig up their bodies for autopsy."

"But cremation is very common these days," Greylock protested. "There's even an unfortunate joke in my profession: 'We make money the modern way—we *urn* it.'"

Canova didn't get the joke, so he ignored it.

"Are you telling me you gave Mrs. Beamer the idea to toast her husband's body?"

"Certainly not!" Greylock stood and walked from behind the desk. "My own feelings about cremation are quite negative. I prefer a more personal passage out of this impersonal world, preserving the body rather than destroying it."

Greylock crouched next to the *papier-mâché* dog. He put his hand on the thing with an unmistakable look of affection. "I would like to do for all my clients what I did for my faithful Ralph here. When he was alive he was always at my side. As you can see, he still is."

Canova felt queasy. "You mean he's inside there? Dead?"

"Mummified, Mr. Canova. Just like the famous ones of ancient Egypt. Perhaps even a trifle better with the aid of modern technology. Would you like to pet him?"

"No, thanks." Canova glanced uneasily at the closed door behind him. *I'm shut in here with a dead dog and a Looney Tunes undertaker.* At least the door wasn't locked. Was it?

"There's no need to be anxious about Ralph, Mr. Canova. You're probably thinking of the so-called curse of Tutankhamen, or perhaps Boris Karloff in the Mummy movies. All nonsense. Mummification is simply a way to preserve the body in recognition that the spirit lives on. Many Egyptian mummies are still in excellent shape after two thousand years, defying the final insults of nature. And I myself have made modern improvements in the formula."

"You mean like, a jigger of this, a jigger of that, and poof, there's your martini—I mean, mummy?"

Greylock laughed, showing teeth almost the same color as his pale face. "It's a little more complicated than that. Soak the body for two months in wine, herbs, and chemical preservatives, coat it with scented oils—jasmine, in Ralph's case—then wrap it in a cocoon of linen, fiberglass, polyethylene, and plaster. For Ralph I added a thin coat of 23-carat gold on the outside."

"I'm sure he appreciates it," Canova said. "He'd probably like it even better if you mummified a fireplug for him. What was that about doing for your clients what you did for Ralph?"

Greylock gave Ralph a loving pat and stood up from his crouch. "Unfortunately, I don't have any clients for mummification yet, Mr. Canova, but I have a dream. This is what it would look like."

He motioned Canova to a watercolor drawing on the wall behind the desk. It showed a pink pyramid with two oversized marble mummies standing guard outside.

"A new kind of mausoleum," Greylock explained. "Instead of crypts, it would have open space for viewing upright mummies. Picture it, Mr. Canova: Row after row of perfectly preserved bodies standing erect through all the ages. Death without decay!"

Canova found the idea of spending eternity upright about as appealing as getting turned into a fancy jar full of ashes. He really needed a cigarette.

"Are you actually going to build that thing?"

"Not soon. I'm afraid it's rather capital-intensive and it's my own project—the corporate ownership of Eternal Rest in New Jersey has nothing to do with it. However, you don't have to wait until my mausoleum is built to ensure yourself a spot. You could get in a reservation now for only five hundred dollars."

Such a deal! "And how much is the rest of the works going to cost?"

"About another seven thousand for the process. Then the sarcophagus is twelve thousand if you go the simple stainless steel route. But I could put you in jewels and gold for a hundred and fifty thousand."

Canova, too numbed by sticker shock to respond for a few moments, didn't like the gleam in Greylock's blue eyes. He felt like he was being sized up for a casket—or maybe for a mummy cocoon. He closed his notebook and returned it to his pocket. "I'll think about it. And if you think of anything that Mrs. Beamer did or said that struck you as odd, please call the number on my card."

"Of course," Greylock said with a little bow of his head. "Anything to be of help."

"Thanks." Canova stood up. As he turned to leave, his eye fell once again on the mummified dog. He looked away. "Tell me the truth, Mr. Greylock: Doesn't it give you the willies to be around dead bodies all the time?"

"On the contrary, it's very rewarding work. As a young man I wanted to be a doctor, so I could save people's lives. It only took me a year of medical school to see that doctors can't do that. They can only postpone the inevitable. Death is waiting for all of us. I try to make it a pleasant experience."

"Right." Canova backed out of the office. "Yeah. Well. Have a nice day."

He turned and stopped just short of bumping into the metal desk occupied by Maisie Wandstradt. When she saw Canova, she took a pamphlet with bright colors on slick paper from her desk top and held it toward him.

"I really think you should read this brochure, Mr. Canova. Preneed planning will bring you peace of mind."

NINE

YOU'RE ASKING A LOT

"Mr. Finn," Hilary Kendrake said, "I've been going through these bills that have piled up. The telephone company is threatening to cut off service, Thrifty Office Rental wants my typewriter back, and Kinko's is going to turn you over to a collection agency. What should I do?"

Finn put his feet on his desk. "Bring me the field reports on the Beamer case."

"About the bills, I mean. I could call these people and negotiate new repayment schedules, if you like. You should save enough each month on long distance and on business insurance to cover the cost."

"What happened with the insurance?"

"Nothing yet, but I know I could shop you a better rate."

It was Monday afternoon, less than a week after Kendrake had first walked into his office and she was practically taking over his business. That chafed. And yet, how could Finn complain? He was already used to having her as an assistant and sounding board through those long hours when they were the only ones in the office. She was more than a secretary to him—in a professional sense. Kendrake was always thoroughly professional, even when she was wearing, as now, a lacy white blouse and khaki skirt instead of a regulation dress-for-success suit.

"Whatever deals you can cut will be fine, I'm sure," Finn told her. "Now let's look at those reports."

On her side of the desk, Kendrake opened a folder.

"Shadd Davis picked up Mrs. Beamer's trash, as assigned, but he got picked up himself by the Delhi Township police in the process. Something about not having current license plates on a truck that didn't belong to him. On the way to the police station the

Beamer trash became mixed up with the neighbors' and Mr. Davis couldn't figure out which was which. He had to throw it all away."

"What was he doing with the neighbors' trash—starting a collection?"

"I didn't follow that, but here's the report. The spelling and vocabulary are rather creative."

Finn accepted the document without comment and gave it only a casual glance. The "garbage gig," as Davis insisted on calling it, was one of his favorite ploys. If only the lad had marked the Beamer trash bags with surgical tape to keep track of them it would have worked beautifully. Hadn't he covered that in Lesson Five? Finn was disappointed. Perhaps Davis didn't have the sleuthing potential that Finn had believed.

"Mr. Funderburgh," Kendrake went on, picking out another report, "spent all of Thursday and half of Friday talking to neighbors of the Beamers. They all agreed that Viola was the perfect wife, protective of her husband and unusually attentive. Mr. F. wrote up separate notes on each interview."

Finn put his feet on the floor and smacked his desk. "She is one of the most cold-blooded killers I've ever come across. It's obvious what she was doing, isn't it? She knew before she married poor Beamer that she was going to bury him in short order, so she made sure their married life was nothing but bliss. If anybody ever started asking questions, there'd be nothing suspicious on the domestic front. The woman's a genius of the homicidal arts!"

"I bet she also saw to it he enjoyed being pampered at home, so he wouldn't develop any nosey friends," Kendrake said. "Neighbors say the Beamers never went anywhere and they never had any visitors except Viola's son by a previous marriage."

Kendrake handed Funderburgh's neatly typed report to Finn. He was thinking hard. He had a feeling that he just heard something that should be setting off alarm bells in his head. But what? The answer was elusive as fog.

"Finally, and most impressively," Kendrake said, "we have the documentation of everything Rosalee Chandler told us on Friday afternoon. It's the only solid lead we have."

"Or need," Finn added, his unease shoved aside. "Five elderly husbands, five quick deaths, five cremations. That should be enough to satisfy our client. Even Canova was suspicious." His face clouded over. "I don't suppose God's greatest gift to woman-kind has bothered to file a report?"

Kendrake shook her head, sending those soft wheat curls splashing over her shoulders. "Nothing in writing. He did leave a message on our answering machine over the weekend. Want to hear it?"

Taking Finn's sigh for assent, she flipped the playback switch on the machine.

"Canova here," came the familiar voice. "Talked to Samuel Greylock, director of the Eternal Rest Funeral Home. Man's a weirdo, wants to mummify stiffs like the ancient Egyptians did, only better. I barely got out of there without getting wrapped in bandages myself. Greylock says there was nothing suspicious about Mrs. Beamer, and he claims that cremation is hot right now. Hot, get it?" The clang of a fire alarm erupted in the background. "Gotta run. I'll file a report later. Over and out."

Finn stared at the answering machine. "I told him to be subtle, so what did he do? He asked the funeral director if there was anything suspicious about the widow. I should never have given him that assignment. And he still owes me a report on the Hawley Smoot business for Cheviot Mutual. We can't tie up Calvin's case and get paid without it."

Finn needed that money more than even Kendrake knew—to help cover a check he had already mailed for the past-due rent.

"Do you want me to get Mr. Canova on the phone?" Kendrake asked.

"No." Finn sank back in his chair. "Get me Norris Beamer."

* * * * *

Within the hour—an hour that Kendrake used to negotiate over the phone with two of Finn's most demanding creditors—the savings and loan manager once again sat where he had the previous Wednesday. This time Kendrake was in the room to take notes.

"My new executive secretary," Finn had introduced her. "Executive" sounded good, he thought; "temporary" did not.

"The reason I asked you to come over," Finn said as Beamer lit his first menthol cigarette, "is that I want you to know we have some indications of a case against your stepmother. Premeditated murder."

"Terrific!" Beamer's caterpillar mustache wiggled. "That you found evidence, I mean."

"It's circumstantial, but strong. We should have the comprehensive written report to you in a few days, but I wanted to give you our findings orally, so you wouldn't have to wait."

Finn took a deep breath. "The primary fact we've uncovered that should be of interest to the police is that your stepmother has been widowed five times under nearly identical circumstances."

He laid out the details—the similarity of jobs among the five elderly men Viola had married, the lack of local survivors to raise a fuss, the cremations assuring that the bodies couldn't be autopsied later. At the end he asked Beamer, "Any questions?"

"Just the big one: Is this kind of stuff going to convince the police and prosecutors?"

"It will get their attention," Finn hedged. "There's still police work to be done. Then if your stepmother is convicted of killing your father, Ohio law says she can't inherit under his will or benefit from his insurance. That's to your advantage as the next of kin. I've already convinced the Cheviot Mutual Insurance Co. to delay payment on your stepmother's claim based on what we turned up."

"That's wonderful!" Beamer said. A long cigarette ash dropped on his pants. He flicked it away absent-mindedly. "What happens next?"

"When we send you our written report you can do with it what you want. I'd recommend you take it to the police."

"And you just step out of it?" Beamer was clearly disappointed.

"The A-Plus Detective Agency has done what you hired us to do, Mr. Beamer. We've uncovered some damning evidence which, while not conclusive, strongly indicates that your stepmother is at worst a killer and at best a fortune hunter."

"Yes, of course, I can see that." Beamer dragged on his cigarette. "I'm just worried that the police will keep this on the back burner. They aren't going to be in any hurry to hop on a murder that's several weeks old and with the body already cremated, are they? Not when you don't have any hard proof. Because if they open a file and then can't prove a case, it just adds to their number of unsolved homicides, right?"

Finn wanted to tell Beamer that he watched too much television, but somehow the detective couldn't bring himself to lie to their client in front of Kendrake.

"Well, it's not impossible the police would think that way," he conceded.

"And how long can this insurance company hold up paying my stepmother if she isn't arrested?"

"Maybe as much as a few months."

"That's not too encouraging."

Finn squirmed in his seat. "What would you like this agency to do, Mr. Beamer?"

"Stick with the case." Beamer crushed his cigarette in Finn's "We're hot on the trail!" ashtray. "Get so much evidence on that woman that even Rufus McCorkle couldn't get her off."

McCorkle was a flamboyant defense attorney with a talent for self-promotion.

"You're asking a lot," Finn said.

"But we'll do it," Kendrake put in.

Finn, stunned beyond speech, stared into her violet eyes. Such intelligent eyes, such compassionate eyes. What the hell did the woman think she was doing?

"Great," Beamer said. "I know this will cost me, but I consider your fee a good investment. Keep in touch."

He grabbed Finn's hand, shook it, and was out of the office before Finn figured out a diplomatic way to overrule Kendrake's acceptance of the nearly-impossible commission.

Kendrake broke the silence in Beamer's wake.

"That was dumb of me, wasn't it?"

"Yes," Finn growled.

"I'm sorry, Mr. Finn. I know it wasn't my place, but I just got carried away. You really need the business."

She crossed her legs. Finn averted his eyes from that distracting sight, focusing instead on the A-Plus Detective Agency fly swatter atop his desk.

"Mrs. Kendrake, I do not believe you understand the disaster you have just visited upon this agency." Finn swallowed. "You have virtually obligated us to secure a conviction in a case where we can't even prove there was a crime. At this point I see no way of doing that short of a signed confession—preferably written in Viola Beamer's own blood."

TEN

GETTING PERSONAL

"I think you're being much too pessimistic, Mr. Finn." Kendrake tugged at her khaki skirt. "If you don't mind, I have a few suggestions."

Finn closed his eyes, took a deep breath, and counted to ten. His head pounded. Really, this was intolerable. For all her competence, Kendrake was a secretary—a *temporary* secretary. What qualified her to suggest *anything*, let alone how to bring a murderess to justice?

"Does that mean you don't want to hear my ideas?" she said, as if she had read his thoughts.

Now she trying to imply that he was closed-minded!

"Don't be ridiculous, Mrs. Kendrake!" Finn thundered. "Never let it be said that Francis Aloysius Finn refused to listen to any well-meaning suggestion, no matter how impractical. But don't you have a lot of filing to do?"

Kendrake rose from her chair and left Finn's office without another word. Had he unwittingly offended her? He was about to call her back when the phone rang. Kendrake answered it.

"Herman Schaeperklaus," she announced on the intercom in tones of tundra-like frigidity.

Finn's landlord. He'd probably tried to cash that rubber rent check. Finn had to hold him off until he could get the money from Cheviot Mutual to cover it.

"Tell him I'm sick or out of town or something, Mrs. Kendrake. I can't chat now. I have to, uh… talk with you. I want to hear your suggestions on the Beamer case."

Within a few moments, Kendrake returned with a newspaper under her arm. It was that afternoon's freshly printed *Cincinnati*

Post. She spread it out on Finn's desk, turned to the classified advertising section.

"Read a few of these 'personals,'" she said.

Finn never wasted his time with this section of the paper. So it was with puzzlement on his round face that he read:

> DWF—41, attractive, loving, sincere, but chubby, 5'2". Seeks SWM for companionship. I'm not perfect so you don't have to be either.

DWF? Five-two was short, certainly, but hardly a dwarf. Finn was mystified.

"Somehow I don't feel any closer to proving that Viola Beamer is a multiple murderer," he observed.

"Read a few more, just to get the flavor."

Finn glanced at the top of the second column, where his eye was caught by:

> DWPM-N/S—38, attractive, charming, discreet, seeks WPF N/S 40-60 with same qualities for occasional rejuvenescent lunch; riverfront restaurant, possibly room service.

Fascinated by the salaciousness lurking in the fine print of his afternoon newspaper, Finn continued down the page without further encouragement from Kendrake:

> WPF—43, tall, tan, trim. Seeks special WPM 40-50. Energetic who enjoys nature, fine dining, travel & a lady with a good mind & great legs.

> SWM—41, seeks dominant WF, would like someone to share like interests, would like to hear from other submissives.

"You don't have to read them all."

"Eh? Of course not." Finn looked up from the newspaper. "You've broadened my horizons with a keen new insight into human nature, Mrs. Kendrake. But what do these pathetic cries for help have to do with Viola Beamer?"

She leaned forward, hands on Finn's desk. Her perfume was breathtaking. "We could use the 'personals' to set a trap for her. An ad that would describe just the sort of man that she's married five times already. If she saw it, she might find it irresistible."

Finn sat back, ruminating. "Suppose she answers the ad. Then what?"

"Then we provide her with somebody who should be the man of her dreams—Mr. Funderburgh. He fits the pattern of her previous husbands perfectly."

Scarcely a moment's reflection was required for Finn recognize that Kendrake was right. Viola specialized in retired government workers, and Funderburgh had been a letter carrier. He wouldn't even have to fabricate a background.

"I don't suppose we could get him to marry her," Finn mused.

"Holding her hand now and then might be enough for him to find out something." Kendrake moved her hair out of the way with a flip of her head. "Mr. Funderburgh is observant and meticulous. If he courts her long enough she's going to make a fatal mistake sooner or later—fatal for her, I mean."

How unfair and unkind Finn had been to Kendrake in his earlier thoughts. He mentally apologized.

"There's a touch of brilliance in that, Mrs. Kendrake," he said, overpraising for good measure. "Let's get Mr. Funderburgh in here."

* * * * *

Funderburgh looked like a model in an ad for a Florida retirement community. His white polo shirt, white slacks and silver hair all contrasted handsomely with his tanned skin. He was trim and fit and probably the best-looking sixty-nine-year-old Viola Beamer would ever see.

"Let me be sure I understand the assignment," he said, sitting in the chair Norris Beamer had vacated a few hours previously. "You want me to place an ad in the newspaper, seeking a romantic partner and describing myself in a way to attract Mrs. Beamer's interest. If she answers the ad I'm to woo her, hoping to get close enough to see or hear something linking her to the deaths of her husbands. In particular, we're interested in the demise of her most recent spouse, Otto Beamer."

"Exactly," Finn said.

"And there is an element of real danger, correct? I mean, the woman is a quintuple murderess."

"Y-e-s," Finn acknowledged with a side glance at Kendrake, who was writing on a legal pad. "I suppose we can't deny that."

"Excellent. I'll do it."

Finn relaxed. "I knew we could count on you. Let's work on the ad. What qualities about yourself do you think would be worth mentioning in the 'personals?'"

"Well, I am happy to say that I have all my own teeth."

"I'm not sure—"

"If you gentlemen don't mind," Kendrake said, "I have some thoughts. In fact, the only part I haven't figured out is the coding at the beginning of the ad. Would you describe yourself as single, widowed, or divorced, Funderburgh?"

"I've never been married."

"Smoking or non-smoking?"

"He's supposed to be looking for a woman," Finn interrupted, "not a seat in a restaurant."

"I don't smoke," Funderburgh said, directing his answer at Kendrake.

Kendrake made a final squiggle with her pen and said, "All right, listen to this: 'SWM-N/S—75, vibrant, retired postal worker, seeks SWF 50-60 for serious long-term relationship involving quiet evenings and few outside distractions. Likes to be pampered.'"

Finn nodded. "That should bring her running."

"But I've never been pampered by anyone in my life," Funderburgh objected.

"We're fibbing about that part, Mr. F.," Kendrake said. "The idea is to make you sound like the sort of person who would fall for the mothering wife routine she used on Otto Beamer."

"That makes sense, I suppose. But I am *not* seventy-five years old!"

"She likes them older," Kendrake said. "Probably because the older he is, the less suspicious it looks when he dies."

"Not that we're going to let her kill you," Finn put in hastily.

Upon this point Funderburgh was immovable, however. In the "personals" ad that appeared in Cincinnati's two daily newspapers on Tuesday, the age of the SWM-N/S looking for "quiet evenings and few outside distractions" was sixty-nine.

By Wednesday, two more of Kendrake's ideas for trapping Viola Beamer were also moving forward.

ELEVEN

DON'T BUG ME

Dick Mobarry whistled a nameless but cheerful tune as he tooled along toward Viola Beamer's house in the western suburbs. It had been a wonderful surprise when Finn called and asked him to plant the bug. Apparently they now had enough dope on the dame to make it worth tuning her in.

Until now, Finn had never shown the slightest interest in the electronic marvels of the twentieth century. The turnabout was a bit of a puzzler. But Mobarry squandered little of his precious brain mass mulling Finn's motivations. He was just glad he had been asked to do what he wanted to do ever since joining the Famous Detectives School: put his knowledge of electronic surveillance to work.

Mobarry was not an electrician or the manager of a Bugs R Us store. He and his wife owned a catering company with forty-six employees. But for years he had been fascinated by the sort of electronic eavesdropping gadgetry that he first became acquainted with back in his days as a low-ranking army intelligence officer in Vietnam. He subscribed to *Popular Science*, *Popular Mechanix*, *Popular Communications*, and *Monitoring Times*. His library of twenty-four books consisted of titles like *Tune in On Telephone Calls* and the *Cellular Mobile Telephone Guide*. He went to electronics trade shows and he bought tons of equipment—none of which he had ever used for anything more exciting than listening in on that teenager next door talking hot sex on the cordless telephone while she sunned herself in a bikini.

Now Mobarry had a task worthy of all that gear in his Dodge RAM van.

Finn had given Mobarry a free hand in his choice of electronic tools. The only important thing, Finn had stressed, was that he get the low-down on Viola Beamer, and that he not get caught. Mobarry himself wasn't willing to settle for one out of two, so he had given the choice of bug a lot of thought. Maximum reliability, minimum detectability, that's what he needed. Mobarry surveyed the options from the exotic (a camouflaged camera hidden in a light fixture) to the mundane. He ultimately settled on the mundane: a six-hundred-dollar infinity transmitter. The beauty of this baby was that his target would watch him install it.

Mobarry was dressed in dark blue pants and a light blue shirt with a home-made Cincinnati Bell patch sewn on the sleeve. It looked like a uniform if you didn't look too closely, and most people wouldn't. When his own phone was worked on just two weeks before, the repairwoman hadn't even worn a uniform. But Mobarry couldn't count on Viola Beamer, who worked at night but ought to be up by now, to buy that. Anybody who'd iced five husbands and gotten away with it had to be a little cautious. It was going to be hard enough convincing her that the phone needed work.

He parked the van several doors away from the Beamer house and walked down, tool box in hand. It wouldn't do for Mrs. Beamer to notice that the vehicle didn't have the familiar Cincinnati Bell logo on it. Nor could he let her see the van sitting there while he eavesdropped.

He rang the doorbell. If she were like most third-shift workers Mobarry knew, Mrs. Beamer stayed awake in the mornings and saved her sleep for the late afternoons. That's how he'd timed his visit, anyway. Waiting for her to answer, tension tightened his gut. Stage fright. He looked around at the aluminum and brick houses. Across the street an elderly woman walked a dog. *Nice neighborhood*, he was thinking as the door behind him opened.

Mobarry's first sight of Viola Beamer came as a shock. He had imagined her as a hatchet-faced woman whose glance could curdle milk. In reality, she wasn't bad on the eyes. She had an oval face with soft features, including an upturned nose and full lips. The short hair framing her face in curls was a warm shade of chestnut, probably dyed. She had plucked her eyebrows. Her fingernails and the toes sticking out of her sandals were painted red. Standing at the door, Mobarry towered over her.

"Phone company," he announced. "We had a report—"

"Come on in," she said in a voice that showed the roughness missing from her body. "Phone's in the kitchen."

This is too easy, Mobarry thought as he followed her through a short hallway.

Viola's hot pink blouse was tied into a knot at the midriff, showing a firm, flat tummy. The legs beneath her white short-shorts were smooth, tanned, and free of veins. A neat little package, about five-foot-five. She looked nowhere near her reported age in the mid-fifties except maybe for the wrinkles at her neck, and they were partly concealed by a gold necklace with a pendant.

In the kitchen, Mobarry was impressed by the central island and the imitation woodgrain cabinets, all newer than the rest of the house.

Viola Beamer pointed to the baby blue wall-phone hanging just inside the door with a bulletin board and notepad above. Mobarry, well trained in the observation techniques of the professional sleuth, noticed that the top page of the notepad contained a name, *Doug*, and a phone number written in ink. Finn would want to know who this Doug was.

"It fades in and out," Viola said. "Sometimes it dies right in the middle of a conversation, like my car phone when I drive under a bridge. I think it must be something in the wiring."

Mobarry nodded, barely able to resist an ear-to-ear grin. "We'll see." *What a stroke of luck!* This murderous cutie had been expecting a repairman from the phone company, and here he was. It could be days before the real guy showed up. Meanwhile, Mobarry would be listening.

"Probably your farbinger, ma'am," he said, tossing off the last name of a kid who worked for him in the catering business. Mobarry didn't know anything about phones except how to turn them into bugs. "Won't take long to fix."

He pulled the phone off the wall, feeling for a second like he imagined a surgeon must feel holding a patient's heart outside the body. Viola watched him with an intimidating intensity. Sweating, even though the AC was chugging away, Mobarry unscrewed the phone and pulled out its wire guts. He nodded wisely.

"Yep, the farbinger, all right." He pretended to take something out. "Luckily, I've got a fresh one with me."

From the tool box Mobarry pulled out an infinity transmitter, so named because this quarter-inch beauty could go on forever using the power from a phone or electrical outlet. It would pick up conversations within a 30-foot radius of the power source. The area behind an electric switch plate was a favorite hiding place, but Mobarry had chosen the phone so he could use the old repairman ploy to get into the house. How right he had been!

As he was slipping the transmitter into the bowels of the phone, Viola wandered away. Mobarry set down the phone long enough to rip the second page off of the notepad on the wall. The impression of the phone number on the page above it could be lifted from that, Mobarry figured, and it could turn out to be important. He'd seen that happen dozens of times on TV.

He stuffed the paper into his shirt pocket and finished installing the bug.

"There," he said, hanging the phone back on the wall as Viola returned to the room. "That didn't take long, did it?"

"Two minutes to do the job, two days to get here," Viola snapped with some exaggeration.

"Sorry about that, ma'am." Mobarry gave his most apologetic smile. *When you're frying in the electric chair, you're going to wish you'd never seen me, you killer bitch.* "We've had a backlog of service calls."

She picked up the phone to make sure there was a dial tone, then showed Mobarry the door—none too soon, as far as he was concerned.

Inside his van he punched up Viola's phone number on his cellular phone. As soon as it rang he blew a whistle into the receiver. That would short out the ring and activate the infinity transmitter. Most of Viola's first floor had just become a broadcasting booth. But anybody who tried to call Viola while Mobarry was tapped in would get a busy signal. If Viola tried to call out, she'd get a dead line. Mobarry chuckled at the thought of the unkind words she would unleash on her incompetent telephone repairman in that case.

He pulled out his egg sandwich and Thermos jug of coffee for breakfast as he settled back to listen to the Viola Beamer Show on his speakerphone. Every hour or so he moved the van to avoid notice, but always within a block or so of the Beamer house in case he had to follow her somewhere.

For a homicidal maniac, the woman led an incredibly dull life, dominated by television. When Mobarry first tuned in, around nine-thirty, she was watching Phil Donahue interview a man who wanted his body frozen when he died. (*Great*, Mobarry thought. *Corpsicles*.) Jerry Springer and the sexual fantasies of Little People followed on the same station. Then Viola switched channels for Geraldo Rivera and some kind of wrestlers. *It can't get any worse than this*, Mobarry thought. Wrong! After a half-hour of local news, accompanied by intermittent sounds of lunch-fixing in the kitchen, Viola started on the afternoon soaps. Mobarry used the wide-mouthed plastic bottle, thankful for Finn's stern lecture on the subject, then ate a ham sandwich. Midway through the sandwich he decided to pass the afternoon trying to count the acts of adultery and fornication on Viola's daytime dramas. He was up to four adulteries and seven fornications—and certain that Viola must be going to sleep before long—when her doorbell rang.

Mobarry sat up straighter.

"Yeah?"

"Cincinnati Bell, ma'am—here to fix your phone."

Mobarry jerked his head up and looked down the street. *Holy shit*, there was a Cincinnati Bell service truck, a white Econoline van, parked in front of Viola's house!

"Boy, you people can't get anything straight," Viola's voice came through Mobarry's receiver. "Another man was here this morning. He already fixed the damned phone."

"That can't be right. The job list is computerized and you were the next one up."

"I don't care what the computer says, I'm telling you a repairman was already here this morning."

"You ought to be careful who you let in your house, ma'am. Why don't you just let me see your phone anyway—so I don't get in trouble with my boss, okay?"

Mobarry, horrified yet fascinated, could imagine Viola turning purple. "Two days it takes you to get here at all, and then you send two people? You're worse than the Post Office, you know that?"

The voices got louder as the murderess and the man from Cincinnati Bell moved out of the hallway and approached the infinity transmitter in the kitchen.

"The man this morning said the problem was in the farbinger."

"What the hell is that?"

"Are you sure you know what you're doing?" Viola demanded.

"I bet there's nothing wrong with your phone at all. It's probably in the wiring."

"That's what I thought, but the man this morning took the phone apart."

"Oh, he did? Maybe I'd just better do that myself."

Mobarry had the sinking feeling that goes with an unstoppable disaster, like when you know the new kid on a catering job isn't going to show, you just know it... and he doesn't.

The next few seconds, which seemed like minutes, passed in silence. The van was like an oven and Mobarry had to pee again. Then the transmitter erupted in sound.

"Criminy, lady! You see that little doodad, right there? You know what that is? It's a bug, that's what. No shit. You got bugged by that phony repairman."

"Can you get rid of that thing?"

"Easy. I'll pull the bastard right out and—"

The transmitter went dead.

Mobarry turned over his engine and stepped on the gas.

TWELVE

UNDER COVER

Dick Mobarry was not in class that night to hear Finn lecture on "Equipment: Cameras, Electronics, and More." Nor had the caterer-cum-sleuth phoned in an oral report on his attempt to bug Viola Beamer's house.

Optimist though he was, Finn couldn't shake off the fear that Mobarry had been caught in the act. Such felonious behavior on the part of an "employee" operating under Finn's PI license could cause that license to be revoked. Worry dogged the detective all during his lecture on the proper tools for gathering evidence without getting hurt. The specter of losing his license, and his business, was only part of Finn's angst. There was also guilt: Dick Mobarry had put trust in Finn's skills as a detective and a teacher, never mind that Mobarry was mostly seeking an excuse for his voyeurism. Now he might be heading for jail as a result.

And for what?

Finn wasn't even convinced that bugging Viola Beamer would do any good. Electronic eavesdropping worked well in organized crime cases because they involved conspiracy, which almost always required that several people talk about the crime. But with whom would Viola Beamer discuss the murder of her husband? Kendrake felt sure that she must have a partner or boyfriend, so Finn had gone along to make both her and Dick Mobarry happy. He remained skeptical, however, and now he regretted ever signing on to his temporary secretary's dubious plan.

Kendrake hadn't come to class tonight. Well, that was all right; it wasn't a job requirement. But Finn found himself wishing she were there at the end of the lecture when the students clamored to talk about the Beamer case. Both those who had an assignment in the case and those who didn't seemed interested.

"So, did that lady waste her old man or not?" The spikey-haired Mary Sue Barkeloo punctuated the question with a pop of her pink bubble gum.

"We believe she did," he responded. "In fact, we believe that she murdered four of the five previous gentlemen to whom she was married earlier."

He summarized the information that Rosalee Chandler had gleaned from court records.

"And let me emphasize," he added, "that Ms. Chandler has provided us with a textbook example of what you can learn by following the paper trail."

Chandler modestly concentrated on doodling in her notebook until Finn urged her to the head of the class to explain how she'd uncovered Viola Beamer's multiple marriages.

"It was really just routine," she said with a shrug, standing at the blackboard. "But I guess that's what detective work is."

She wore a green cotton dress, belted, that set off her auburn hair and stopped about three inches short of her kneecaps. The dress hiked up at the back whenever Chandler reached to write on the blackboard in retracing her steps through the county bureau- cracy and other sources of information. Joe Canova watched her with all the interest of a woman-eating shark, Finn noticed. The firefighter's eyes continued to follow Chandler as she took her seat and Nelson Funderburgh, at Finn's request, rose to talk.

"I visited the Beamers' street twice, knocking on every neigh- bor's door," Funderburgh said. "I was invited to watch television, barked at by a Rottweiler named Snake, and permitted to dice onions for an omelet, among other adventures. But I didn't learn anything negative about Viola Beamer—unless you want to hold it against her that she didn't mix much with the neighbors."

Again, Finn had the feeling that something in Funderburgh's written report was fishy or out of place or just didn't add up— something that he missed. He shook it off.

"As a matter of fact," Finn said, "I do hold it against her that she was so unsocial. It's highly suggestive under the circumstances. So is the testimony from the neighbors that she was extraordinarily attentive to her husband."

"You mean she was, like, fattening him up for the kill?" Barkeloo asked. *Pop!*

Finn cringed. "She was attempting to deflect in advance any possible suspicion from herself. The police may not be persuaded of that, but I am."

When Funderburgh resumed his seat, Finn added, "We have, of course, pursued numerous other avenues of investigation—without notable success, I regret to say."

He thought of Dick Mobarry's dubious assignment, fate unknown, and decided it would be wiser not to mention it to the students. Instead, Finn forced a sheepish Shadd Davis and an unbowed Joe Canova to speak for the edification of the class. Davis's presentation of his adventures with the Beamer trash was something in the hyper manner of Eddie Murphy, whereas Canova leaned more toward the Joe Friday style as he told about his interview with Samuel Greylock. At the end, looking toward the lovely Chandler, Canova insisted on describing his clever use of a video camera in the insurance fraud case.

"Solid work, Mr. Canova," Finn acknowledged, "but please don't forget the written reports you owe me."

"Oh, yeah," Canova said without any noticeable embarrassment. "Got them right here."

He handed the typed papers to Finn, who was almost prostrated by the realization that he would actually have to read the stuff. But with Canova's documentation Finn could close that insurance fraud case, get paid by Cheviot Mutual, and finally get Schaeperklaus off his back about the rent.

"Class dismissed," he announced.

As the class broke up, Funderburgh came up to Finn with a hesitant look on his face.

"I hope you aren't worried about this business of your ad in the 'personals,'" Finn told him before he could say anything. "You may start getting replies to your ad as soon as tomorrow."

"Not at all." Funderburgh dismissed the mere notion of worry with a wave of his hand. "I'm rather excited, actually." He looked around. "I couldn't help noticing that Mrs. Pertwee wasn't with us tonight, Mr. Finn. I hope she isn't ill."

"Rest assured, Funderburgh, she isn't ill." Finn closed the door of the classroom behind them. "She's on a special assignment in the Beamer case. Under the covers, you might call it."

How can I keep this up? Viola Beamer asked herself as she trudged down the tiled hallways of the Hanging Gardens Retirement Center.

The floor was cracked, the walls were dingy, and the lights did more to cast shadows than to chase them away.

Who would ever suspect that a woman who worked in a crummy place like this was worth nearly a million dollars? That was why Viola stayed on the job at a succession of sleazy rest homes long after she had to work at all—it was a perfect cover. Plus, she made some easy money on the side dabbling in sales of stolen pharmaceuticals.

But now that it was almost over, she could barely stand being around all these old people. They talked crazy, they drooled out of the sides of their mouths, and they had to be pushed around in wheelchairs. Wasn't it bad enough that she was always married to some geezer who wasn't in much better shape?

No more of this crap. After her death, she would split for Mexico and never look at an old man again. The million, wisely invested under five different long-established identities, was all the money she needed. She'd live like a queen south of the border— a queen bee, that is, with lots of worker bees. Handsome young matadors would be nice.

Humming at the thought, Viola ignored a female resident wearing a night gown and tennis shoes, a cloth doll clutched to her shrunken breast.

She turned left, into a small room. The decor looked like that of a hospital slated for demolition: industrial bed, faded blue curtains, artificial flowers on the plywood night stand, and a color TV with fuzzy reception. At least the white-haired woman lying in the bed didn't have her mouth hanging open or her face twisted into a grimace. Maybe this one could even take a leak without help.

"You're new here, aren't you, honey?" Viola said.

"Yes, I am. I arrived yesterday, but I believe you were off." Smiling, the woman extended a hand. "My name is Alice Pertwee."

THIRTEEN

PARTY LINE

Outside the nursing home, Dick Mobarry stifled a yawn. He wasn't used to getting up at five-fifteen in the morning, as he had to in order to be waiting for Viola Beamer when she got off work.

The chain of thinking that landed him here began almost as soon as he'd skedaddled from Cherry Tree Lane in his van. With the bug discovered, Viola would be spooked for sure. So what would she do next? If she had a boyfriend or an accomplice, this would be one time she'd almost certainly feel a need to contact him—or her. *Hey, somebody's on to us. Somebody planted a bug!* And she'd be afraid to call from home until she had a chance to have the place searched for more bugs. So would she call from a phone booth? Maybe. Then Mobarry remembered Viola's casual reference to a car phone. That would be a cellular phone. Everybody seemed to have one these days, thank God.

Mobarry stopped home to trade the van for his Toyota Camry and pick up his Icom IC-R7000, a thousand-dollar scanner that would pick up cellular phone calls. Monitoring such calls was illegal, unlike Mobarry's pastime of eavesdropping on cordless phones. But the law was one hundred percent unenforceable and could be violated with scanners costing as little as two hundred bucks.

Picking up random calls was a cinch. One of Mobarry's biggest kicks came the time he scanned on to a guy's cellular call telling his wife he had to work late—followed by a call to his girlfriend saying he was on the way.

Tuning in to a particular call and keeping it wasn't so easy, though. The signal was constantly handed off to different cell towers and different frequencies. But Mobarry thought he was adept enough to catch at least part of Viola's cellular conversation if he followed her car and locked on to the call as soon as it began.

He trailed her last night from her house to the nursing home, but she made only one call from the car and got no answer. Maybe she'd try again on her way home from work. Now it was six a.m. and she should be coming out... Yep, there she was—one of three or four women coming out the back entrance. She was heading toward her four-year-old white Escort. Mobarry turned his key in the ignition.

Taking no chances that she would notice him, Mobarry waited until Viola was close to leaving the lot before he eased his Camry out of its parking space. Just as he turned onto the street, two cars behind her, he saw Viola put the car phone to her ear. Mobarry fiddled frantically with the dials of the scanner, until he heard a familiar steel-wool voice.

"...tried calling you last night, but I didn't get any answer."

Got her! Viola Beamer, no question.

After the initial thrill, Mobarry realized with chagrin that he had missed the first few words of the call, when names might have been used.

"I stepped out for a few minutes." It was a man's voice. "Why didn't you call back?"

"No chance. They're watching me too closely. Never mind that, we're in deep shit. Somebody tried to bug my house."

"What! What do you mean, 'bug?'"

Use his name, damn it, Mobarry thought.

"I mean just like in the movies—a little transmitter planted in my kitchen phone. A telephone repairman found it and took it out."

"How did it get in there to begin with?"

"Some big fat guy was here earlier in the day, posing as a phone man."

I'm not fat! I have big bones. Mobarry, enraged at Viola's description of him, momentarily lost control of the car and had to swerve to avoid colliding with a Ford Ranger.

"...put it there," Viola was saying when Mobarry returned his attention to the scanner. "Beamer's son must be behind..."

The voice faded out. Mobarry worked the dials feverishly until he heard—

"...rid of that digitalis?" The man's voice.

"What do you think, I'm brain dead or something?" Viola retorted.

"Just being careful. We have to…"

Gone again.

Mobarry was still trying to lock back on to the call when, less than a minute later, he saw Viola a couple of cars ahead of him hang up her phone.

FOURTEEN

LOVE NOTES AND DRASTIC ACTION

That morning, some hours later, found Finn reading Joe Canova's overwritten reports on the insurance fraud case and on his interview with Samuel Greylock of the Eternal Rest Funeral Home.

The one for Cheviot Mutual Insurance was primarily a formality backing up the videotape. It gave the date and time that Canova observed the subject discard his cane to fix a flat tire. Finn made a few changes with his pen to tone down the Spillanesque prose, gave the report to Kendrake to retype, then settled in to read about Greylock.

Having already had two oral reports from Canova—on the answering machine and again in class—Finn held out little hope that he'd find anything of interest in the written version. But one never knew, so Finn soldiered on through such writing as:

"Subject is a white male, thirty-six to thirty-nine years old, approximately six-foot-one, one hundred and ninety pounds, dark brown hair, bearded."

Finn conceded Canova points for the details.

"Upon questioning by investigator, subject asserted that Mrs. Viola Beamer betrayed no unusual nervousness or other suspicious behavior while arranging or attending her husband's funeral…"

Finn cringed as he remembered Canova's bull-in-a-china-shop approach which yielded that assessment from Greylock. He was supposed to have been subtle in questioning the funeral home director.

"Subject informed investigator that cremation is growing in popularity, with about seventeen percent of human carcasses toasted annually. Subject himself, however, displayed obsession with mummification as means of dealing with cadavers. Most graphic representation of this was the presence in his office of a mummi-fied Great Dane covered in gold leaf. The canine's name is Ralph."

For the love of Sherlock Holmes, what did the dog's name—

The intercom on Finn's phone crackled. "Mr. Funderburgh is here to see you, Mr. Finn."

"Send him in, Mrs. Kendrake."

How refreshing, Finn thought, not to have people just barging into his office. He offered silent thanks for Kendrake's presence and her professionalism.

She followed Funderburgh in, carrying a stack of manila and letter-sized envelopes.

"Responses to my ad in the papers," Funderburgh said, point-ing to the mail. Pride tinged his voice. "Twenty-five on the first day."

"There are a lot of widows out there," Finn said. "Let's see what we've got."

All three began opening envelopes.

One of the fatter packages came from a real estate agent who sent one photo of herself and several others of houses she'd sold. She was also built somewhat like a house, her portrait indicated. Enclosed was a resume reminiscent of a Multiple Listing Service description. ("Believes in building a solid foundation for a lasting relationship…")

Another respondent included a letter of reference from a previ-ous gentleman friend. ("She is not good at lying, leading people on, or seeing more than one man at a time. Also bakes good apple pies.")

Funderburgh was raising his eyebrows at one letter and Finn was chuckling at another when Kendrake exclaimed, "Look! Here's one on Hanging Gardens Retirement Center stationery. Isn't that where Viola Beamer works?"

Finn tore the envelope out of her hands and ripped it open.

"Dear SWM-N/S," he read aloud. "You sound like the com-panion I have so sorely needed since my dear husband (God rest his soul) passed on. I can't promise to pamper you until I know what you mean by that, but I may be just the person you'd like to pass those quiet evenings with. You'll never know unless you meet me at noon Friday inside the front doors of Krohn Conservatory. I'll be wearing an orchid and carrying our lunches."

The letter smelled of lilac water. It was signed with a row of X's and the letters "SWF."

"Fascinating," Finn said. "This is just like watching a spider spin her web."

"A black widow," Kendrake put in. "Surely this letter is from Mrs. Beamer."

"I haven't been on a date in thirty years," Funderburgh said. "What should I do?"

"Be on time," Finn said. "Make it clear you have a good pension and no heirs. Advance the relationship as fast as you can; there's no danger of scaring this one off. And be prepared to deliver a full report later, as usual."

Funderburgh's military posture became more pronounced. "I'll do my best, Mr. Finn."

"It seems a shame," Kendrake said, "not to open the other letters." She had several in her hands.

The ringing of Finn's phone short-circuited whatever comment he might have contributed. Kendrake answered.

"A-Plus Detective Agency. Oh, hello. Yes, he's right here."

She cupped her hand over the mouthpiece and whispered "Dick Mobarry."

Finn grabbed the phone.

"Are you all right, Mr. Mobarry? Did you get caught?"

"Not quite. And I know how she killed him—digitalis."

"Where did you get that?"

"From the lady herself. I'm not going to mention her name on an unsecured line, but you know who I mean. I picked her up talking to a man on her car phone this morning. She told him about the bug in her kitchen and he said the dead guy's son was probably behind it. Then he said something about digitalis, and I know about that stuff. It must have been how she did away with her husband."

"Think hard, Mr. Mobarry. What exactly did this gentleman caller say about digitalis?"

"Sorry, the reception on the scanner was fading at that point and I only caught a few words. 'Rid of the digitalis,' I think it was. Then she came back with something like, 'You think I'm brain dead?' It was like maybe he'd asked her a question and that was her answer. They finished talking before I could pick them up again."

"Damn."

"Sorry," Mobarry repeated.

"Don't be. I'm pleased that you've done so well, Mr. Mobarry. If anything else that might be significant comes to you while you're writing your report, call me."

When he'd hung up the phone, Finn pulled a pseudo-Havana cigar out of the top right drawer of his desk, where it had nestled next to his Victoria's Secret catalog.

"I've never seen you smoke," Kendrake said.

He sensed a health lecture coming.

"I only indulge when I'm thinking hard." He lit up. "Right now I'm thinking, 'Why would Viola and a co-conspirator be talking about getting rid of the poison *two weeks after the murder*?'"

Finn related Dick Mobarry's end of the conversation to Kendrake and Funderburgh.

"I can't believe that Viola's playmate was telling her to destroy the evidence of poison only now," he added. "She's not stupid. She would have done that before the body was even cold."

"Maybe her friend was just double checking that she had," Kendrake suggested. "And because it was so obvious, she made the crack about not being brain dead."

"Perhaps. Yes, that must have been it."

"But I don't understand this business of digitalis being a poison," Funderburgh said. "I have a friend who takes it and it doesn't kill him."

"That's because he has a bad heart," Finn said. "Ironic, isn't it? Drugs of the digitalis series are used to regulate heart rhythm in people who have congestive heart failure. But an overdose to a healthy person increases the flow of blood to the heart so much it can induce a fatal heart attack. You might say the heart beats itself to death."

He leaned back in his chair. "Otto Beamer had no known heart problems—I confirmed that with the insurance company earlier. So if there was digitalis in his house, it wasn't prescribed for him. That would be strong circumstantial evidence of foul play."

"But it must be long gone," Kendrake pointed out. "You said that yourself."

"There could still be traces left behind—a fragment of a label, an unwashed medicine bottle, something like that."

"If there is now, I bet there won't be by the time we could talk the police into a search warrant. Viola's been put on her guard."

"There's the rub," Finn agreed. "We need to take some drastic action quickly."

He smoked, letting his eyes wander across the top of his desk. It was cluttered with reports—from Rosalee Chandler, from Nelson Funderburgh, from (at last) Joe Canova.

Canova. Insurance fraud. Hawley Smoot.

As his mind made the connection, Finn's face split into a smile. "Or better yet, let's get somebody else to take action."

FIFTEEN

BLACKMAIL IN A GOOD CAUSE

Finn didn't even try to conceal his contempt for Hawley Smoot.

"Hawley," he said, "calling you a low-life doesn't begin to do you justice. Vermin like you give degeneracy a bad name. You would be at the bottom of the social order in any county jail in this country. Even your three-dollar wig is crooked."

Smoot unconsciously touched the hairpiece. "What's this all about, Finn? I didn't have to come here and be insulted."

"True. You could have been insulted anywhere—the public library, for instance."

Smoot's bulldog jowls sagged further. He blinked his mournful eyes at the detective.

"Jeezle, Finn, you never let up. I pay my taxes, I go to church every Christmas, I root for the Reds. But I made one mistake in my life…"

Smoot's put-upon demeanor, which seldom failed to win sympathy from empathetic judges, left Finn unmoved.

"Hawley, you tried to suck a lady's toes right in the middle of the library," he said, almost shouting. "That's what I call sick."

"She practically asked for it. She was wearing sandals, wasn't she?"

"The woman was a Franciscan nun, you pervert."

"I didn't know that until the trial. Why don't they wear habits, like when I was a kid?"

Finn wondered what Kendrake would have thought of Smoot's pathetic comebacks, but she wasn't there to hear them. The detective had sent her home early. He didn't want her to be an accomplice before the fact to what he was going to force Smoot into.

"That toe business was the lowlight of a long career." Finn held up a sheet of paper covered with handwritten notes. "I have the details right here, having called some friends in the law enforcement community just to refresh my memory. I count twenty-five arrests, eighteen convictions."

"Okay, so I made more than *one* mistake," Smoot muttered.

"And you got an early start at it. I'm sure you recall fondly your first brush with the law at the age of nine. You were sent to reform school for burning down your own house because your mom wouldn't let you sleep overnight with a friend. The friend was a girl."

"It wasn't my fault. I was a mixed-up kid. I came from a broken home."

"You probably broke it, Hawley. To continue: At the tender age of fifteen you took up what must have seemed to you a promising trade for a boy of your talents—burglary."

"I got caught the first time out," Smoot said.

"That's what they all say. In your sorry case, I can believe it. You must have gotten better at it, though, because you only had two more burglary raps as an adult. Of course, you also did time for auto theft, picking pockets, selling marijuana, and that disgusting episode in the library. You were a major contributor to the prison overcrowding problem, Hawley. Then you became an entrepreneur, kind of like me."

Smoot smiled at this recognition that he and Finn were, after all, brothers under the skin.

"That's when those humorless federal authorities noticed you. They took a dim view of your innovative efforts in Florida condo sales. Mail fraud, they called it. How was Joliet, by the way?"

"It stunk."

"I would have thought an out-of-shape, defenseless hairball like you would have been popular with the boys at Joliet."

Smoot shuddered. "I was."

Finn was enjoying this. "And now you're back in Cincinnati using a different name."

"That ain't illegal. I checked."

"Not unless it's done in furtherance of a crime—say insurance fraud, for example. I want you to watch something with me."

Finn pointed at the rented television behind Smoot. As Smoot turned to face it, Finn pushed a button on the remote in his hand.

The Hawley Smoot Show kicked into life and rolled on for the next ten minutes. At the end of it a visibly shaken Smoot licked his lips.

"It was a miracle cure," he said. "I went to Lourdes and got healed. I just didn't get around to telling the insurance company yet."

"Then how do you explain still using the cane when you came in here?" Finn asked.

Smoot sighed. "Are you doing this just to torture me or do you really want to cut some kind of a deal, like you said on the phone?"

"Both. First of all, can we agree that at minimum this tape voids your claim with the Cheviot Mutual Insurance Co. and at maximum proves you're guilty of insurance fraud?"

"Yeah, yeah, you got my ass in a sling. So what's the rest of it?"

Finn smiled. "I'm willing to destroy the tape. What's the matter? You look pale."

"You're not making that offer out of the goodness of your heart, Finn. You got no heart. You must want something out of me. Something godawful."

"Nothing that would violate your slimy moral code. I just want you to break into a house. Tonight."

"What is this, some kind of entrapment?"

Finn leaned forward. "You've already been trapped, you fool. I've got you by the balls and I haven't even begun to squeeze yet. As much as it sickens me to think of it, I have a dirty job to do and I don't know of anybody dirtier than you to do it. If you come through, I promise to destroy that tape. And you know I'm a man of my word."

"That's blackmail," Smoot protested.

"Absolutely. But in a good cause. This may be the only noble thing you've ever done in your whole miserable life, Hawley."

"Finn, I ain't done night work in years. Besides, I'm too old for that kind of stunt."

"You're twenty years younger than you look and the job isn't difficult. The target is a three-bedroom home in a modest neighborhood, not Fort Knox. Security should be minimal. The woman who lives in the house works at night, so it's certain no one will be there when you come calling."

In truth, Finn was risking more than Smoot in this contemptible deal. He was throwing away, at least temporarily, the sure thing of his much-needed fee from Cheviot Mutual in return for getting the goods on Viola Beamer—and the favorable press that would go with a successful murder case. It was a bold gamble that only an entrepreneur could make. Kendrake wouldn't understand at all. She'd be too worried about the overdue rent, if she knew about it. Finn was worried, too, but he had to risk it. He didn't get into this business just to feed Schaeperklaus. He wanted the big time.

"What's the scam?" Smoot asked.

"The woman murdered her husband. We have reason to believe she poisoned him with a heart drug called digitalis. The purpose of your visit is to find some trace of that."

"You mean like a half-empty bottle?"

"Not a chance. This woman also killed four previous husbands and got away with it, so she isn't witless. But there could be some remnant of the bottle, or the label, or even the receipt of purchase. Check the medicine cabinet and the bedrooms. And don't overlook the trash—she knows someone is on to her, so she may have thrown something out just today."

"You don't expect much, Finn. What am I supposed to do if I find something—waltz it in to the cops and stay to make a confession while I'm at it?"

"Hardly. Evidence of the digitalis is only damaging while it's in that house. If you find any with the killer's fingerprints all over it, you're going to plant it elsewhere in the house. Somewhere she won't see it and discard it. Then I'll arrange to get the police there with a search warrant."

With a sense of shame, Finn recognized the expression on Smoot's face as admiration. Had Finn sunk that low, to be admired by Hawley Smoot?

"So you want me to frame the broad for a crime she actually committed," Smoot said. "How cute! But what happens if she's already ditched every trace of that digitalis stuff and I don't find nothing in her house? That's not my fault. What happens to the tape then?"

If he made the deal contingent on success, Finn realized, Smoot would calculate his chances at close to zero and figure he'd be better off bolting.

"Just bring me back something from the house that proves you were there and you're off the hook."

Smoot stroked his jaw. "I ain't as dumb as you think," he said at last. "I know you ain't doing this yourself because you're afraid you'll get caught. But what about me? I'm a human being, too—"

"That's debatable."

"—and what happens if *I* get caught? With my record, they'll throw away the key."

"Then you'd better not get caught, Hawley. Look, the choice is yours: Accept my offer and you run the risk of a little trouble. Turn it down and your insurance scheme definitely goes down the tubes—and you with it. Don't kid yourself that Cheviot Mutual won't report this to my former employer."

"What about *your* risk, Finn? If I do get caught, you think I won't tell the cops who sent me?"

Finn snorted. "And do you think any law enforcement officer in his right mind would believe a slimebag like you?"

"Damn you, Finn. You got all the angles covered, just like when you worked for the prosecutor." Smoot sighed. "Where is this house you want me to hit?"

SIXTEEN

THE UNLUCKIEST S.O.B.

He was, Hawley Smoot reflected, the unluckiest son of a bitch in the world.

Case in point: Any other guy would have been believed when he claimed he was only bending down to tie his shoe that time in the library. But for some reason the library cop took that nun's word over his. And the woman was wearing a denim skirt instead of a habit over her nicely turned ankle! Now that just wasn't fair.

Neither was his current woe—caught in the clutches of Francis Aloysius Finn just because that bastard happened to be working for the insurance company involved in his accident claim. Smoot thought the personal injury scam would be a breeze. Like semi-retirement. Now, thanks to Finn, he was back to burglary.

He had one thing going for him, he thought as he drove across the dark county roads toward Cherry Tree Lane—the faithful EP-007 Executive Lockpick Set in his breast pocket. It looked like a fountain pen until unscrewed, revealing an assortment of thin pieces of metal with the necessary crooks and bends to open locks. Just having a thing like that could put a man with his record back behind bars for a long time. But Smoot's professionalism demanded he use proper tools.

At three o'clock in the morning, Cherry Tree Lane was a graveyard. Smoot drove down the street, then parked around the corner. He walked the half-block to 823, making little noise in his black gym shoes. All the homes looked alike in the dark, except for the one ranch-style house. The numbers painted on the curb in front of each house told Smoot which was the right one. Passing a line of trash cans set out for the weekly collection later that Friday morning, he went down the driveway to the back of the house.

At the back door, thoughtfully left unlit, Smoot went to work with the EP-007. Manipulating two pieces of metal in the lock while wearing latex gloves wasn't the snap it appeared to be on all the crime shows. Standing there on the back porch, feeling exposed despite his dark clothing and the lack of a porch light, Smoot could have sworn it took an hour to wiggle those tumblers into place. His hands were sweating inside the gloves and acid churned in his stomach. He was more out of practice than he'd thought.

Later on, Smoot figured out that he'd actually passed only ten minutes on the porch, if that, before he heard a satisfactory click. The door opened into a kitchen. Smoot returned the lockpick to his pocket and pulled out his flashlight. He aimed it low so it would illuminate the room without shining through the windows. Nice cabinets, Smoot thought. Almost like real wood. His own domestic arrangements over the years had been such that he'd seldom had a bathroom of his own, much less a kitchen, but he appreciated class when he saw it.

Now for the trash can Finn wanted him to go through. Had to be in the kitchen somewhere. Smoot swept his flashlight around. Table and chairs. Stove, refrigerator. Nowhere did he see a trash can. Must be hidden inside all that cabinetry somewhere. Smoot started opening doors beneath the metal sink. Skillets in one. Pots and pans in another. Stacks of paper bags. A brown plastic trash can. Bingo! Smoot's luck was finally changing. But when he removed the can from the cabinet it felt light enough to be empty. Okay, another break. If there was only one thing in there, say an empty bottle, that eliminated Smoot's problem of not knowing what he was looking for and how to recognize it when he saw it. He opened the lid of the trash can and shone his light down into the plastic trash bag inside.

Nothing. The damned thing was empty.

The owner of the house probably changed bags earlier that day, when she set out the big trash cans in front of the house for collection. Shit! Damned if he would rattle those metal babies out in the street at this time of the morning, looking for God-knew-what. But how to get out of it and still con Finn into destroying that videotape? Easy, Smoot told himself with a smile after a moment's thought. Just bring in proof that he'd been in the house. That's all Finn demanded. Why risk his neck doing anything more? He should have thought of that in the first place.

With the flashlight sitting on the floor, shining toward the sink cabinet, Smoot used both hands to put the trash can back where he'd found it. That was when he saw the skull and crossbones.

The universal symbol of poison was affixed to a cylindrical container wedged beneath the sink pipes. Smoot set down the trash can and picked up the container. The label was written in scientific words Smoot didn't understand, but he caught the dire warnings IN CAPITAL LETTERS. He focused on one word: ARSENIC.

His mind reeled. This was the best possible proof that the woman who lived here, whoever she was, had killed her husband. Why else would she have arsenic in her kitchen cabinets, for crap's sake? But it wasn't the proof that Finn wanted, that digi-something heart drug. Well, Finn was wrong about the murder method, that's all. All the better. Smoot could save his own ass and make a fool of his old enemy in the process.

Wait a minute. Maybe he could do better for himself. He had the poison right in his hand. Why not find out who lived here and put the squeeze on her? Saving her from a Murder One rap ought to be worth thousands. *I'll just take the arsenic and let Finn think— No, dammit. That wouldn't work.* As Finn had said, poison didn't prove anything unless it was in her house. And if it was in her house, Smoot couldn't use it to blackmail her because she could just get rid of it. *I'm still the unluckiest—*

Hold on. Smoot saw another way to get something worth money out of this deal. It would only take five minutes to grab a few rings and necklaces that would be easy to fence. What harm could an extra five minutes do? Finn would never know.

Smoot made a thirty-second search of the downstairs: dining room, family room, living room, no bedroom. He climbed the stairs, regretting a twinge of arthritis in his right leg. Finn would never believe it, but there were days he really did need the cane. If he ever had to run for it, he'd be a goner.

The first room on the right at the top of the stairs was sparsely furnished with a single twin bed. Smoot figured it for a seldom-used guest room.

As he shone his flashlight on the first room to the left, Smoot caught enough of the bed to see that it was at least a queen-size, maybe a king. That was the room he needed.

Not until he stepped into that room did Smoot see the body sprawled across the bed. It was a woman. Dark red, drying blood from a gaping hole in the side of her head was spattered over her white uniform and the pink bedspread.

Fighting back the bile in his throat, Smoot moved closer. He pulled one of the ragged threads off his shirt and set it on her nostrils as he'd seen done on TV. No motion. She wasn't breathing.

It just ain't fair, Smoot mentally screamed to himself as he ran out of the bedroom. *I am the absolute, no-contest, unluckiest son of a bitch in the world.*

SEVENTEEN

IN THE STILL OF THE NIGHT

In the dream, Finn wore a bowler hat and an Edwardian suit and carried an umbrella. Kendrake wore a red jumpsuit with a white stripe down the middle. They were engaged in a stylish battle with the Positive-Negative Man, a villain whose touch carried twenty thousand volts of electricity. The juiced-up crook reached out his metallic finger to touch Finn and—emitted a crackling sound. The sound turned into a ring.

The telephone.

"*Mrs. Kendrake, we're needed.*" The words were in Finn's head as he awoke, the dream breaking into real life.

Finn sat up, leaned across his bed, pulled the jangling phone off the nightstand.

"Finn," he announced in a sleep-soaked voice.

"This is Smoot. We got problems."

Finn looked at the glowing red digits of his clock radio. 2:36 A.M. "What problem could be so big it couldn't wait until the rooster crows?"

"The lady is dead."

"What lady?" Groggy *and* grouchy.

"The poison lady. You never told me her name."

Finn put his feet on the floor, fully awake now. "You killed Viola Beamer? I ask you to do a simple burglary and you have to—"

"No, no, it wasn't like that, Finn. She was dead when I got there, I swear. You got to help me."

"Help you? I don't even know you."

As Smoot screamed Finn's name the detective moved to hang up the phone, then realized that wouldn't be wise. If Smoot were facing an aggravated murder charge, the prospect of having his home video turned over to Cheviot Mutual Insurance Co. would hardly be enough incentive to keep Finn's name out of it. And despite what Finn had told Smoot about the police disbelieving a multiple felon, they would at least investigate—and learn that Finn had made inquiries about the victim.

What a mess. Finn was getting sucked into the wrong end of a murder case and his financial woes seemed further away from resolution than ever. Unless...

Unless he could somehow get a client out of Viola Beamer's demise. Doubtful, but not impossible. Finn always lived in hope.

"All right, Hawley," he said. "Calm down. I'll help you. Never leave a man behind. But first we have to meet somewhere so you can tell me everything that happened. I don't want to do this over the phone." He thought for a second while Smoot poured out his pathetic gratitude under the delusion that Finn cared what happened to him. "Where are you?"

Smoot, calling from a phone booth, named the intersection.

"Meet me at the Delhi Kroger store," Finn said. "It's open all night. You can be there in five minutes. It'll take me less than ten."

"Why don't I just meet you at your place?"

"Because I still don't know you."

Finn hung up. As he pulled on pants and shirt he struggled to recall the dream that had been shattered by the phone call. Something warm and pleasant... Ah, yes. A plot from the old *Avengers* TV series, with himself recast as the impeccable John Steed and Hilary Kendrake as his delectable companion, Mrs. Peel. That's what Smoot had interrupted, damn him. Finn would make him pay for that.

* * * * *

Inside the brightly lit grocery store it was hard to believe it wasn't broad daylight outside except for one thing: the lack of customers. Finn wandered down one empty aisle after another looking for Smoot, worried that he had been arrested or gone to the wrong store. Finn finally found the con man in the beer and wine section.

As Finn approached, pretending to study wine labels, Smoot held up a bottle. "Here's a nice little Chablis. Saucy but not too impetuous."

Finn jerked it from him and casually glanced around. The aisle was as empty as Smoot's brain. "Tell me about the body," Finn murmured, his eyes on the label of the Gallo wine.

"She was on a bed upstairs. Probably shot. Blood everywhere. Real creepy in the light from my flash."

"What were you doing in her bedroom?"

"Looking around. You know."

"I can guess. There's a classic scenario for you—shot in her bedroom by a burglar. That's what the police will think. How do I know they won't be right?"

"I didn't see any signs of a burglar."

"You were the only burglar, you dolt! If I know you—and I do—you decided to grab a few valuable souvenirs for yourself while you were there. Suppose she caught you at it and you killed her?"

Smoot appealed to Finn with his most hangdog look. "Like you say, Finn, you know me. I never hurt nobody, did I? I don't even know how to use a gun."

"Come to think of it, you'd probably shoot yourself if you tried." Finn sighed. "And if you killed her you'd be half way to Oshkosh by now instead of standing here with me. All right, I'm persuaded you're innocent. A first. How was the victim dressed?"

"In white. Almost like some kind of uniform."

"She was ready for work, then." Finn put down the California wine and picked up a bottle of Meier's Lake Erie La Brusca Rosato. "She worked from nine-thirty at night to six in the morning. It would take her a half hour to get to work, which backs us up to nine o'clock. Viola was killed sometime between getting dressed and nine o'clock. You mentioned using your flash. Were the lights off all over the house?"

"Yeah."

"Then either it wasn't dark when she was killed or the murderer turned off the lights, which seems pointless. It's been getting dusky around eight-thirty of late. So I suspect she died around eight o'clock."

Finn wanted a cigar as he calculated the implications of Viola's murder for his client. They weren't good. It might be harder now to prove the woman's guilt in the death of Otto Beamer. And neither Viola's inheritance from the old man nor her insurance blood money would automatically pass to Norris; they would become part of her own estate. Norris would have to sue the estate to get the money that was rightfully his.

Who had killed Viola, and why? Something to do with her own murderous history? Finn couldn't imagine what, but like all detectives he was suspicious of coincidences. For Viola and her husband to both be murdered without some connection would be a coincidence indeed. Maybe if Finn could solve this murder he would at the same time pick up evidence against Viola that would help his client. Tenuous, very tenuous. Still—

"That don't help me none," Smoot broke in. "I don't have an alibi for eight o'clock, either."

"You mean you were out committing some other malfeasance?"

"I happen to have been out with a lady friend, wise guy," Smoot said with dignity.

"So why isn't that an alibi?"

"What I mean is, I gave her twenty bucks and she was my friend for twenty minutes. We didn't get around to exchanging names."

"I hope she had nice toes," Finn said. "You did wear gloves tonight, didn't you?"

Smoot pulled them out of his pocket and held them up.

"Good. Never discard rubber gloves at the scene of the crime. Sometimes the police lab can lift prints from the inside. Take those gloves home with you and nobody can prove anything." Finn narrowed his eyes. "Unless you took something from the house."

"Just one thing." Smoot's melancholy visage turned smug as he added, "The poison."

"What!" Only by tremendous force of will did Finn avoid shouting. "You found it?"

"Excuse me." A middle-aged woman in a white lab coat cut in front of Finn and picked four bottles of Harvey's Bristol Cream off the shelf.

"Yeah, I found it," Smoot said when she'd disappeared down another aisle. "Only 'it' ain't what you think. First place I looked for any sign of that heart drug you talked about was the kitchen trash can. No dice. But when I put the can back under the sink I found something even better. Arsenic."

For a moment the unexpected word was a sound without meaning for Finn. "That's not how she killed her husband," he said finally.

"Don't look a gift horse in the ass, I always say. Arsenic looks just as bad against her as digiwhatever. Maybe she was going to use it on somebody else."

"You're inventing this, Hawley. No killer would be stupid enough to leave a can of arsenic sitting around the kitchen. Especially not when she knew somebody was on to her." He picked up a four-dollar bottle of André Champagne.

Smoot shrugged his droopy shoulders. "Maybe it sounds goofy, but it's true. I not only saw a container with a skull and crossbones on it, I had that sucker right in my hands."

"Did you hide it in the house, as I told you to do with the digitalis?"

"That's where I kind of messed up, Finn. See, I'm still carrying the poison when I find the corpse. I run out of the house and I'm not much thinking about arsenic. I'm out to the sidewalk before I look down and realize I've still got it. Can of poison in my hands, bloody corpse in the house behind me. Don't look too good, right? So I pull the lid off a garbage can sitting at the curb and cram the arsenic way down into one of them plastic trash bags."

Finn set the Champagne on the shelf with a thud. "So the poison is conveniently lost. I knew it, Hawley! You made up this whole cockamamie story to explain why you don't have any proof of being in the house."

A look of near-panic took over Smoot's lugubrious features. "But I was there, I swear it. You'll have your proof when somebody else finds the body and this murder is all over the news tomorrow. How else would I know about it if I wasn't there, huh? I did what you wanted and you owe it to me to get rid of that tape. A deal's a deal."

"We'll see."

Driving home, Finn still didn't believe Smoot's story about the arsenic. It was against Finn's principles to ever believe Smoot, for one thing, and it was a totally implausible tale for another. But why had Smoot told it when his knowledge of the murder would be enough to convince Finn that he'd been in the house? Habit, perhaps? Or could it, incredibly, be the truth? That would be easy enough to establish with a look inside the trash cans in front of the Beamer house.

Just two blocks from home, Finn made a U-turn in the empty street and headed back toward Viola's neighborhood.

At the top of Cherry Tree Lane he put on the brakes. Down the street, by Viola's house, flashing blue and red lights illuminated the night. Police cars. Finn backed up and drove home, staying carefully within the speed limit.

His sleep the rest of that night was fitful, haunted by dreams that had nothing to do with the *Avengers* and that he had no wish to remember the next day.

EIGHTEEN

THE MORNING AFTER MURDER

Dick Mobarry was on his way to work Friday morning, listening to police calls on the scanner, when he heard:

"...think so. I'm leaving the scene of that homicide on Cherry Tree Lane." *Holy shit—a murder on Viola Beamer's street!* What if it was her?

Mobarry redirected his car toward Delhi Township and called his wife, who was already at work at Annie's Catering, to tell her he'd be in late.

"Are you screwing around chasing police calls again?"

"Ease up. I'll be there in twenty minutes."

The night before he tried to tune in on Viola's car phone again. Finn always said that luck favored the persistent. But after waiting an hour and not seeing the white Escort pull out of her garage, he decided he must have just missed Viola leaving for work. The Escort hadn't been in the rest home parking lot, either. He figured then that Viola must have had the night off.

Now she was dead, or one of her neighbors was, and Cherry Tree Lane was crawling with cops. Mobarry saw the Sheriff's Department cruisers as soon as he turned onto the street.

Two or three of the black-and-whites were parked in front of the Beamer house. A deputy sheriff stood on her front walk, putting his walkie-talkie back on his belt. So it was Viola Beamer who was dead, or at least her house that was the scene of murder. Mobarry would drive by, see if he could catch sight of Viola inside the house. Finn would expect that.

There was a car in front of Mobarry, a yellow Camaro. He'd seen it before, or one just like it, parked a couple of doors away from the Beamer house the other day. A neighbor, he'd figured.

By why would a resident who parked at that end of the street be driving on this end at seven-thirty in the morning?

Little things like that bugged Mobarry.

The Camaro slowed almost to a stop as the only person in the car, the woman driving, stared at the commotion in front of the Beamer house. A natural reaction, Mobarry thought. But then she stepped on the gas and sped away, as if she were running from something.

On impulse, Mobarry followed her.

* * * * *

Gus Hackleshin's toast was buttered, his coffee was poured, and his cereal was snap-crackle-and-popping at him. The only thing missing was his morning newspaper. Why was Gloria taking so long to retrieve it off the front lawn?

The thought had no more than formed in his mind before Gus heard the front door open and close. Gloria barreled into the kitchen.

"What's the matter?"

"You won't believe what happened." Her china-doll face was flushed with excitement. "Somebody killed Viola Beamer."

He grabbed the newspaper out of her hand. "Let me see that."

"It's not in there." Gloria sat across the table from him. She was roughly half Gus's size, in every dimension, but never nagged him about his weight, not even at meals. "I saw a bunch of cop cars next door, so I went over and asked what was going on. They said she'd been murdered. Shot. You never think of something like that happening in your own neighborhood, do you?"

"No."

But that friend of Otto Beamer had thought of it. The old man. He'd asked whether Gus had suspected foul play in Otto's death.

Gus took a pill from one of the bottles in the bowl in front of him.

"They'll be asking a lot of questions now, won't they?" he asked. "Poking into her life?"

"Sure." Gloria watched all the true-crime shows on television. "They may even talk to us. Not that we know anything."

Gus felt one of his chest pains. He used to be an honest guy. Why the hell had he ever gotten mixed up with Viola Beamer?

"You look like shit, Mom," Bill Longdale said as he tied his tie. "The bags under your eyes have bags."

"I've been up watching ever since I called the cops. You should have seen 'em take the body away, wrapped in a sheet like they always show on the news. Stick your shirt in, Billy."

It was a tossup as to which was more depressing: Being tossed out of your own home and having to move back in with your mother at his age, or finding out that she hadn't changed a bit and thought that you hadn't either.

He joined her at the living room window. There was still a police cruiser across the street, and a TV3 crew filming the outside of the house. "How long do you think the cops will hang around?"

"Damned if I know."

"The publicity is going to play hell with property values for a while. Who do you think killed her?"

"Some man, I bet." Bessie Longdale squinted at her son. "Were you diddling that woman?"

She thought he balled every woman he knew, that having been his father's habit. In Bill's case she was only half right.

"Don't be silly. My involvement with her was strictly business."

* * * * *

His secretary set a cup of coffee on the desk in front of Richard Chavez. "Isn't that awful about Viola Beamer?"

Chavez, administrator of the Hanging Gardens Retirement Center, took a deep breath and looked up from his paperwork. "What has she done now?"

"Got herself killed. Didn't you hear?"

He shook his head. "Good grief, no. What happened?"

The secretary sat on the chair in front of him, her buttocks hanging over both sides. "It was on the radio this morning. Somebody shot her."

"How horrible." He stroked his pencil-thin mustache.

"Yeah. I guess. But if you ask me, that makes one less problem for you to worry about, Mr. Chavez."

Chavez thought about the argument with Viola in his office—and the expression afterwards on the face of that new resident, Mrs. Pertwee. He was certain she was listening.

And he wondered if the problem of Viola Beamer really was over.

NINETEEN

ANGEL IN DISGUISE

Hilary Kendrake arranged to be off work Friday to take her eight-year-old daughter to Kings Island theme park, north of Cincinnati. It was, she realized, a way of making it up to Amanda for getting a job and leaving her each day with Sandy Rembert. Sandy had three daughters of her own and a swim club membership, but Kendrake felt guilty nonetheless.

And yet, she knew she shouldn't. She loved Amanda dearly, but she had hardly been out of the child's sight, except during school hours, since Bob's murder. It was high time to branch out. That was the whole idea of finally going back to work, although at a temporary job. She wasn't ready for any bigger commitment yet.

But Mr. Finn was so completely disorganized, so out of his depth running the business, that he was helpless without her. He realized it, too, even though she could tell he didn't like it at first when she started giving him her ideas on the Beamer case. It felt wonderful to be needed, for the first time in years, for her professional skills rather than her domestic and maternal ones.

This morning, though, she was concentrating on the latter, making Amanda and herself a breakfast of blueberry pancakes, bacon, and decaffeinated coffee. She paid scant attention when the radio in the background broadcast a brief news report about an overnight murder:

"A Delhi Township woman was found shot to death in her home early today by police investigating a burglary."

Amanda, taller than most boys her age and every bit as aggressive, was rattling on over the crime news. "I can't wait to go on Gravity Zero. Everybody says it's awesome."

Kendrake shuddered, knowing she couldn't stand to watch her daughter's blond curls tossed around by the force of the highly publicized new ride, much less go on it herself.

"Police say Viola Beamer lived alone. An unidentified suspect is under arrest." Viola Beamer! Kendrake spilled coffee on the table cloth instead of pouring it into her mug. "Shhh," she said, interrupting Amanda's graphic description of the self-guided ride's possibilities.

But the radio skipped on to a report of a chemical explosion that had killed one person and injured seventy-two. Kendrake turned it off, the better to think about the Beamer case.

With Viola Beamer dead, all of Kendrake's strategies for getting Viola to condemn herself were doomed. Viola wouldn't be answering Mr. Funderburgh's lonely hearts ad, or going to work at the Hanging Gardens Retirement Center where Mrs. Pertwee could spy on her, or talking to her accomplice on a cellular phone for the enjoyment of the eavesdropping Dick Mobarry.

This wouldn't do at all.

"Mo-om!" Strung out to at least two syllables. "I said, 'May I have another pancake?'"

"Oh. Sure."

Mr. Finn is up to something else, though, Kendrake thought as she poured batter into the skillet. He sent her home yesterday when that Hawley Smoot character arrived, and she received the distinct impression their conversation had something to do with the Beamer case. Well, what was it to her anyway if he didn't want her to know? She was only a temporary secretary in a business that was probably temporary, too. It wasn't as though Francis Aloysius Finn and his antics were important to her.

She tried to dismiss all thoughts of the A-Plus Detective Agency as she caught up on a week's worth of laundry and house cleaning, then packed bathing suits and suntan oil for the park.

But as she and Amanda were heading up I-71 toward Kings Island a few hours later, the noon news update on Kendrake's car radio blew the day's plans out of the water:

"Police have arrested Norris Beamer of Westwood in connection with the shooting death last night of his stepmother, Viola Beamer. She was found dead in her home by…"

Kendrake jerked the silver Volvo to the right, getting into the exit lane.

"Are we there, Mom?"

"No, honey, we're taking a bit of a detour."

* * * * *

At exactly that moment Nelson Funderburgh stood at the entrance to Krohn Conservatory, looking for the orchid corsage that would identify Viola Beamer.

The retired letter carrier hadn't listened to or watched any broadcast news that morning. He'd lingered over coffee and the morning newspaper (printed too late to contain an account of Viola's murder) until a quarter past nine. Then he began preparing for his luncheon assignation.

He showered, shaved, and applied Brut cologne. Now the tricky part. What did one wear to attract a money-grubbing multiple murderess? Funderburgh doubted that style or taste were prerequisites. A suit made of thousand dollars bills might be the most effective. Lacking that, he ironed a pair of khaki pants and a robin's egg blue shirt. He selected a burgundy tie and a navy blazer to go with them. The total effect was rather preppie, he decided with approval as he considered himself in the full-length hall mirror. Did people still say "preppie?" He wasn't sure.

Driving to Krohn, Funderburgh tried to put himself into the part of the SWM-N/S who had written the newspaper ad. ("Believe it and you become it," Mr. Finn advised in Lesson Two.) SMW-N/S was suave, he was debonair, he was lonely and on the make. This would take real acting on the part of a man who cherished by his solitude and his independence. Fortunately, he had years of community theater experience to call upon.

He parked his Dodge Colt in the conservatory lot and entered the glass building, feeling a slight acceleration in the beating of his heart. Normal apprehension, he assured himself, not a malfunction of his pacemaker.

The conservatory, open to the public year round, wasn't as crowded today as when he'd made the traditional Christmas and Easter visits with his late mother. It wasn't difficult, therefore, to spot the woman standing just inside the front door, as promised. Large frame, white hair. That didn't match the description of Viola

Beamer. In fact, from this angle, she looked a lot like someone he knew. If she would turn around—

As though she read his thoughts, she did.

"Mrs. Pertwee! I thought that was you."

"Why, it's Mr. Funderburgh. How pleasant to see you. Do you come here often?"

"It's been years. I have an appointment to meet someone."

He regretted that duty would take him away from what could have been a pleasant chat with Mrs. Pertwee. Then he noticed the orchid pinned to her bosom and the white paper lunch bags in her hand.

"SWF?" he asked.

"I certainly am. SWM-N/S?"

Funderburgh acknowledged the identification with a bewildered nod. What in the world was Mrs. Pertwee doing here instead of Viola Beamer?

* * * * *

Still casually dressed in blue culottes, Kendrake took Amanda with her into Finn's office. The detective was slumped over his desk, chin in hand, his eyes bleary. A sad sight. He perked up the instant he saw the visitors. "Hello, ladies."

"Hi. Just thought you'd like to meet my daughter. This is Amanda. Amanda, this is Mr. Finn."

"Hello," Amanda said. "We're going to Kings Island today."

Finn tried to hide his disappointment, but it was obvious to Kendrake. "Nice of you to stop by." Seated, he wasn't much shorter than Amanda was standing up. "Would you like to be a detective when you grow up, Amanda?"

"No. I'd like to be a lawyer like my daddy, or a nuclear scientist."

"Well, the world could certainly use more of both."

"I heard our client mentioned on the radio," Kendrake said. "Bad news."

Finn nodded. "Events are moving quickly, too. A friend in the prosecutor's office tells me Beamer has already hired Red Dog McCorkle to defend him."

"Then he must be guilty."

"I'm hoping he just has low sales resistance."

Rufus McCorkle, known as Red Dog to Court House intimates, was without doubt the most widely advertised criminal lawyer in the eight counties of Greater Cincinnati. For a time, he had even appeared in commercials for a local weight loss clinic, until he had to quit when he gained back the weight plus interest. In his own hard-driving TV spots he always wore a T-shirt inscribed with his phone number—555-WALK. McCorkle ended every ad by looking at the camera and promising: "If I can't get you off, nobody can!"

He usually did get his clients off on the big charges, even if he had to get them convicted of a few minor ones in the process. McCorkle would do anything to win, as his frequent appearances before the Cincinnati Bar Association's ethics committee attested. But word around the Court House was that many a quieter attorney had a better record of complete vindication for his or her clients.

"Beamer doesn't have any motive for killing his stepmother," Finn added. "What could he possibly gain?"

"Revenge," Kendrake said, watching Amanda wander around the room.

"The police might think so, but he wasn't that broken up about his father's death, remember. If he shed any tears it was over being disinherited. Killing Viola did nothing to remedy that. In fact, it may have reduced our chances of proving she murdered her husband."

"If Beamer doesn't have a better defense than that, he's sunk."

"That's Red Dog's problem. But I would think his best defense is to identify the real killer."

"Then that's what we have to do."

Her tone of voice was meant to indicate the subject was closed. Finn disagreed. "We haven't been hired for that. Nor is it likely we will be, with Red Dog on the case."

The phone rang. Amanda beat her mother to it. "A-Plus Detective Agency. Just a moment, please." She held out the receiver to Finn. "It's for you."

Finn smiled his thanks. "Hello. Yes, Mr. Mobarry. What!"

For two minutes he listened. Then he wrote a series of numbers and letters on a notepad. "You've done better than I could have hoped, Mr. Mobarry. Thank you."

As he cradled the phone, Finn was already explaining to Kendrake: "Mr. Mobarry went back to Cherry Tree Lane this morning. A car that he'd seen parked on the street Wednesday sped away from the scene in a suspicious manner, or least he thought it was suspicious."

"Do you think that was just his imagination?"

"Possibly. But he says the woman driving the car made several swift turns that caused him to lose her." Finn held up the paper on which he'd written. "He did get her license number. If we were on the case I'd call a cousin of mine at the Bureau of Motor Vehicles and find out who owns the car."

"Do it," Kendrake urged. "Then get Red Dog to hire you."

"How am I supposed to do that?"

"Maybe you can't, but Beamer can. He's the client and he likes us. If we failed to find the killer, nobody would blame us, but—"

"We wouldn't fail."

"Then think of the favorable publicity. And the clients that would bring in. And the fees."

Finn smiled and stood up. "Mrs. Kendrake, your argument is compelling. I'll try to get into the case."

Kendrake grabbed Finn's shoulders. "Beamer must still be in custody at the Justice Center. You ought to run down there and talk to him after you trace the owner of the car. Amanda and I will mind the store."

"Oh, Mo-om." Amanda put on the twisted face she reserved for the infrequent occasions she didn't get her way. "What about Gravity Zero?"

"We'll go another day. I promise."

"I couldn't possibly ask you to give up your off-day plans, Mrs. Kendrake," Finn said.

"You didn't. I volunteered. Amanda will adjust."

Kendrake became aware that her hands were still clutching Finn's shoulders. With embarrassment, she let them fall to her sides.

The detective acknowledged neither her action nor her discomfort. "Mrs. Kendrake, you are the most persuasive of women as well as an angel in disguise." He gave her a look that transcended gratitude. "And it's not much of a disguise at that."

TWENTY

RED DOG

Waiting in a Lysol-scented room of the Hamilton County Justice Center to talk to Norris Beamer, Finn felt a twinge of guilt for not telling Kendrake about Smoot's involvement in the case. He kept her in the dark on the early-morning mission to Cherry Tree Lane for her own good, but he still felt sneaky doing so. The woman gave up a day at Kings Island with her daughter to help the A-Plus Detective Agency. He must tell her the whole story as soon as he had a chance.

But for now, he could only sit and ponder such nettlesome questions as: Where did the woman in the Camaro fit into the picture? Finn's cousin at the BMV, Bill Testarosa, had identified the owner of the car—presumably the driver—as Sheila Graf LaFeulle, with an address across town from Cherry Tree Lane. Finn had never heard of her.

When he finally was allowed to see his client, Finn was shocked at the change that had come over the S&L manager. Beamer's face was haggard, washed-out, as if he were a subject of this week's "America's Most Wanted." The authorities had taken away his tie and his suspenders. Just looking at him made Finn feel wrinkled. If there was any way that he could help this man, Finn vowed to himself, he would do it, even if he couldn't talk Red Dog into hiring him.

Beamer was on the other side of a glass partition, able to talk to Finn only through the telephones they each had in front of them. Finn never would have been allowed even this far if he hadn't had friends among the deputy sheriffs at the Justice Center.

"Hello, Mr. Finn." Beamer's voice was tinny over the phone line. "I didn't expect to see you here." He struck a match against a matchbook cover three times before he got it to light. He held it to his cigarette. His hand shook.

"That should be my line," Finn said. "I've been here lots of times. I assume you haven't."

Beamer expelled cigarette smoke in a grim chuckle. "Funny how your life can go topsy-turvy so fast. When I came to you last week the most important thing in my life was getting my inheritance. Now I just want to get out of jail. The cops read me my rights and fingerprinted me, like on some police show. It was humiliating. I can't believe they think I killed Viola."

"You didn't, did you?" Before Beamer could answer, Finn added, "Remember, I'm not your attorney and this isn't a privileged conversation."

"Of course I didn't kill her. I'm no killer—she is."

"Was," Finn corrected. "Why do the police think you did her in?"

"They told me Viola left a letter saying that if she were killed I should be suspected. She claimed I accused her of my father's murder, and that I threatened her."

"And I suppose you didn't do that, either—threaten her?"

"The only time I ever talked to the woman was at my father's funeral—and I certainly didn't threaten her."

Finn rubbed his chin. "This whole idea of a letter fingering you for the murder is just too convenient for somebody. I smell a rat— like a giant rat of Sumatra. How can the police believe that you'd leave a thing like that lying around if you killed the woman?"

"It wasn't lying around. She left it with her lawyer. To be opened in the event of her death."

"Oh. Well, I don't suppose you have an alibi for the approximate time of the murder yesterday?"

Beamer shook his head. "I was home alone. Most of the evening I was watching TV, then I went to bed around eleven o'clock."

"What did you watch?"

Beamer stubbed out his cigarette, fumbling for a memory. "Several shows. I remember one of them was *Mystery* on PBS. Sherlock Holmes."

A rerun, Finn realized. Describing the plot, even if Beamer managed to remember it, wasn't going to convince anybody that

Beamer was snug at home in front of the boob tube during the murder.

"Mr. Finn?"

"Sorry. I was just thinking."

"Have you proved that Viola killed my father?"

"To our own satisfaction, yes. But I don't know what a prosecutor could make of it."

Beamer lit another menthol cigarette from a half-empty pack. "Then why are you here?"

"Because you're a client of the A-plus Detective Agency, Mr. Beamer, and our clients are never left in the lurch when legal problems arise." Finn was ashamed now that it took the prospect of a fat fee and the pressure of his overdue rent to get him to the Justice Center. "I want to help you defeat this scurrilous charge."

"Mr. Beamer has all the help he needs, thank you," said someone behind Finn.

It was difficult to go a day without hearing that gravelly voice on radio or television ads, accompanied by video in the TV version. But Finn hadn't seen Rufus McCorkle in person for months. Finn's 13-inch TV screen scarcely did justice to Red Dog's growing girth. And while his body was getting larger, the strawberry hair that had inspired the "Red Dog" nickname during McCorkle's long-ago days as a rock 'n' roll DJ was thinning.

McCorkle glared at Finn over the top of his rectangular plastic glasses. "What're you doing with my client, Finn, you old pirate?"

"He was my client first. Hello, Red Dog."

Finn shook McCorkle's hand with warmth. He had always admired the lawyer's aggressiveness in the court room and on the airwaves, even though they had been on opposite sides until now.

"Sorry you lost your job at the prosecutor's office," McCorkle said.

Finn shrugged it off. "I could have gone to work for Worldwide Investigations or one of the other big agencies after that, but I wanted to run my own shop."

"So I see." McCorkle pointed through the window at his bedraggled client, who watched the conversation he couldn't hear with a blank expression. "Mr. Beamer briefed me on his suspicions involving his stepmother. Care to bring me up to date on your investigation?"

"Of course. I'm here to help." Using guarded language because of the illegality of Mobarry's eavesdropping, Finn told McCorkle about Viola's cellular conversation with her presumed accomplice.

"Any idea who he was?" McCorkle asked.

"A few possibilities, but we haven't pursued that angle yet. We tried—without success—to locate the digitalis or some remnants of it that we could call to the attention of the law enforcement bodies."

"Tried how?"

"No comment, Counselor. You aren't my attorney, so that wouldn't be privileged."

"You have a criminal mind, Finn. You should have finished law school."

Beamer tapped on the glass, then pointed at McCorkle. Finn handed the lawyer his phone.

"Maybe Mr. Finn could help you find the killer," Beamer suggested loud enough for Finn to hear several inches away. "He already knows a lot about Viola."

When McCorkle looked at Finn, the detective had the distinct impression it was with amusement. "How about that, Finn? Any theories about who might have killed our client's stepmother?"

"Her accomplice, perhaps?"

"Perhaps," McCorkle agreed. "On the other hand, maybe it was just what it looked like: A burglar who got caught in the act, killed the homeowner, and was so frightened by what he'd done that he scrammed without stealing anything."

"But Mrs. Beamer started work every night at nine-thirty. So she had to have been killed before that time—probably in daylight hours. You don't need a coroner's report to tell you that. Are you asking me to believe your burglar broke in by daylight?"

McCorkle shook his head. "No, although that's not so far-fetched and you know it. I'm asking you to believe that the murder occurred much later—in the early hours of the morning. That's when my witness saw the burglar."

With a sinking feeling, Finn grasped that the bungling Smoot must have been spotted. It would mean ruin for the A-Plus Detective Agency if he were caught, Finn's dream a nightmare.

Finn cleared his suddenly-dry throat. "Your witness?"

"I had one of my staffers in the neighborhood asking questions within an hour of my being retained. She got lucky."

Leave it to Red Dog to pull something like that. The joke around the Court House was that he sometimes showed up at the scene of a murder before the victim.

"The neighbor across the street who called the police was willing to talk to us," McCorkle went on. "She heard a noise in the night and looked out just in time to see a man get into a truck outside the Beamer house. She called the police anonymously at two minutes after three. They arrived, found the front door open, searched the house, found the body."

"Just playing devil's advocate, couldn't that intruder have been your client?"

McCorkle smiled as he shook his head. "The dude was black, according to my witness. She didn't mention that in her call to the police, by the way. She was in too much of a hurry to get back to the window, although by the time she did the truck was already gone."

Finn's world turned right-side-up again. A black man—not Smoot, then. And he must have arrived on the scene nearly half an hour after Smoot had left.

"But if Mrs. Beamer was killed in the early morning, how do you explain that she was still home and in her uniform, instead of at work?"

McCorkle shrugged his broad shoulders. "I don't have to explain everything. We operate under a wonderful presumption of innocence in this country, Finn, which means my job is only to raise a reasonable doubt about Beamer's guilt in the minds of the jurors."

"I suppose she could have taken a nap on her bed and overslept," Finn said, half to himself. "Or at least you can suggest as much to a jury, Red Dog. You'd better find that man with the truck before the police do, though. Just in case he's innocent."

"I do like your style, Finn. When I want to find somebody I usually hire Worldwide, but I'm sure you could handle this. Do you want the job?"

"Sure I do," Finn said. "To be honest, I was hoping you would ask."

"Good. Is there anything you need to know?"

"I do have one question for our client." He picked up the phone. "Mr. Beamer, have you ever heard of a woman named Sheila La-Feulle?"

Beamer nodded. "Why, yes. She left a message on my answering machine a couple of days ago, but I was never able to reach her. She said she had to talk to me—'had to' was her phrase—about my father."

TWENTY-ONE

DIRTY WORK

Finn walked in the front door of the A-Plus Detective Agency early that afternoon with a new bounce in his step. Less than an hour on the murder case, he already had two suspects in mind. If one of them turned out to be the murderer, he could save his client from prison, attract favorable attention in the press, and cement a lucrative connection with Red Dog McCorkle.

Mobarry was right about the woman in the Camaro being more than a casual passerby outside the murder scene. She called Norris Beamer before the murder. That made her worth a closer look, at the least. Then there was Red Dog's burglar, who would make a wonderful red herring even if he wasn't the killer.

Sheila LaFeulle would be easy to find through the data on her driver's license. And the fact that Finn had, as yet, no idea how to trace the presumed burglar without a license plate number or even a good description of the vehicle bothered Finn not at all. He would find a way.

Perhaps, in her amateur's enthusiasm, Mrs. Kendrake might even have a workable idea. At least he could ask her, make her feel good. But, to Finn's profound surprise, she was not at her post when he entered the A-Plus office. In her place at the reception desk was her daughter, Amanda, reading a *Star Trek* comic book.

Finn gaped. "Where the h— Where's your mother?"

"At the computer store down the street," Amanda said. "She said she won't be gone long. She's just shopping. There's a man waiting for you in your office. He said you know him."

Shopping? Considering the way Kendrake had nagged him about acquiring a computer, Finn didn't like the sound of that. But he thanked Amanda and headed for his office.

Before he had gone two feet the phone rang. Amanda stretched out her hand for it, but Finn pounced and grabbed the receiver.

"Finn here."

"Oh, Mr. Finn," a woman's voice said. "Is Mrs. Kendrake there?" What was this, a personal call at the office? Kendrake never had one before.

"I'm sorry, she's out. May I take a message?"

"This is Rosalee Chandler. I've finished running the paper trail on those two neighbors of Viola Beamer. I guess you still want them, even though she's dead?"

"There must be some misunderstanding, Ms. Chandler. I didn't ask for a background check."

"But Mrs. Kendrake called and asked me to do it."

"I see." Finn tightened his grip on the phone. "Of course. Mrs. Kendrake called." *What did the woman think she was doing?* "And a very important assignment it is, Ms. Chandler! Well, give me what you have." Under the watchful eye of Amanda, Finn uncapped a felt-tipped pen with one hand.

"Okay. Augustus John Hackleshin is forty-six years old, five feet eight inches tall, weighs three hundred and eighty-six pounds. Former truck driver, but he's been on disability for eighteen years. He suffers from diabetes, emphysema, high blood pressure, and a weak heart. Married to Gloria Stern Hackleshin for twenty-four years. She's a waitress at a new hotel downtown. Nice tips, I bet, but probably not a very good medical plan, if any. I suspect that's why their house has three mortgages on it and all their credit cards are maxed out. Oh, and they have a daughter, Mary, who attends a Catholic high school—Seton."

"Any problems with the law?"

"Not even a traffic ticket for any of the three. The wife and daughter drive a 1979 Maverick, by the way. He doesn't drive. That's all I have on them.

"The man across the street is William Scott Longdale, age forty-two, five feet nine, one hundred sixty pounds. He's been a realtor for twenty years. Made the Million Dollar Club in four of the last five years, which means he's good at it. He was married to Nancy Temple Longdale for sixteen years, but he wasn't so good at that. According to the documents filed in their divorce, he had enough affairs to qualify for an episode of *Sally Jessy Raphael* all by himself."

"Was Viola Beamer's name mentioned?"

"No, but not all his women were. The wife got the kids—they have three—and the house in Anderson Township. The house will be paid off in five years. Mrs. Longdale is a brand manager at Procter & Gamble. None of their credit cards are overextended and both of their cars, a Lexus and a BMW, are paid off. That's it."

"That's plenty." Finn's hand was cramping again. "You've done your usual excellent job, Ms. Chandler. Now I have a new challenge for you: I want you to interview a woman named Sheila LaFeulle. Her car was seen twice in the Beamers' neighborhood, and she tried to call Norris Beamer to talk to him about his father."

"Oh, I just couldn't, Mr. Finn."

"You couldn't? Why not?"

"I don't deal with people very well."

"Of course you do. You get clerks to help you find things all the time."

"That's different."

"No, it isn't. Clerks are people."

Amanda cupped her hands around her mouth. "Mr. Finn," she said in a stage whisper.

"Hold on, Ms. Chandler." Finn pushed the "hold" button. "What's the matter, Amanda?"

"Are you ever going to see that man waiting for you?"

Good grief, he'd forgotten about his visitor. Never keep a customer waiting. "Yes, I'd better do that." Finn got back to Chandler. "Maybe we'll discuss this more later."

"I won't change my mind, Mr. Finn."

"All right, all right, then." Finn hung up and went back to his office. It wasn't a customer he found there. Sitting in one of the chairs, with two black plastic bags on the floor next to him, was Shadd Davis.

"Hey, Mr. Finn," he said, standing up. "I got it." He held up the bags. "That lady's garbage."

"What lady?"

"You know. Mrs. Beamer."

Finn had to sit down. "That assignment was last week, Mr. Davis."

"I went back."

"Obviously. But why? You didn't want to do it to begin with."

"Yeah, man, but I felt like a fool in class, talking about how I messed up. Never goin' to impress my lady Brenda that way, right? So I give it another shot." He yawned. "I didn't know she was dead. Viola Beamer, that is."

"Of course not. And this time you went to her street in the wee hours of the morning, so nobody would see you, isn't that it?"

Davis nodded. "About three A.M. How'd you know?"

"I'm a detective."

So the burglar spotted by one of Viola Beamer's neighbors had been no burglar at all but one of Finn's students. What a mess! The best chance for weakening the murder case against his client lay in throwing suspicion on a student sleuth guilty only of completing a class assignment.

"Did I do good?" Davis asked.

"Great. Brenda should be wowed." No sense in burdening him with Finn's plight. From Shadd Davis's point of view, he had done the right thing. And maybe he had.

"We goin' to check out the trash now?"

Finding proof that Mrs. Beamer had killed her husband, which was the object of seizing her trash, now took a back seat to proving Norris Beamer *hadn't* killed his stepmother. But that didn't lessen Finn's interest in exploring the Beamer trash. Discounting Smoot's lie about arsenic, there was still a chance that a careful search might turn up something—perhaps even something that pointed toward Viola's own killer.

"We'll open the bags," Finn told the eager student, "but not here, for heaven's sake." He thought a moment. "We can do it in the garage at my house, then hose down the garage afterwards. You have gloves, don't you?"

Davis nodded. "I remembered Lesson Three, man."

Good student, Finn thought with satisfaction. He pulled his own pair of plastic gloves out of a lower drawer in his desk.

As he passed through the reception area on their way out, Finn found Kendrake back at her desk and Amanda sticking a manila file folder into a metal cabinet.

"I'll be out for an hour or so investigating Mrs. Beamer's trash." He pointed toward the bags in Davis's hands. "While we're gone, please call Mr. Mobarry and have him talk to this Sheila LaFeulle. She left a message on Mr. Beamer's answering machine that she wanted to talk to him about his father. Have Mr. Mobarry find out why. By the way, you didn't buy a computer while you were gone, did you?"

Kendrake shook her head, sending her hair bouncing. "No, but I want to talk to you about that. They're having a sale. Maybe you could pay cash and you wouldn't have to worry about your bad credit rating. Also, I've been collecting information for you about the various data banks available that could be helpful in investigations. A PC wouldn't be just for my word processing."

"I appreciate that." Finn opened the front door. "But let's see how this case turns out first. We may be able to bill Beamer enough hours to pay some past-due invoices and still get the computer."

"Cool," Amanda said.

"On the other hand," Finn added, "if I lose my license and go to jail, I won't need it."

* * * * *

Finn had opened his business in the suburbs because that's where he judged his retail market to be. Ultimately, he envisioned an A-Plus Detective office in every mall and strip center in America. But at heart he was a city man, and that's where he lived, in the same solid brick house where he had grown up as a boy. It had hardwood floors, stained glass windows, real plaster walls, and nine-foot ceilings. The garage below the house was only wide enough for one car, but that was fine with Finn. He only owned one car. It was to this garage that Finn took Davis.

After parking his Accord in the driveway Finn picked up two fallen tree branches from the back yard, each about the size of a dime in circumference. "Poking sticks," he explained. "There are probably things in those bags we won't want to touch, even with gloves."

Davis spread newspapers on the floor of the garage, which was spotless, then put down the two plastic bags and opened them. The mild odor told Finn there wasn't any maggot-infested food inside, which was a blessing.

"We'll use the sticks to spread out the contents," Finn said, slipping into his lecture mode as he put on gloves.

There were boxes and bottles and cans—and lots of paper.

"Put all the paper to one side," Finn ordered. "I want to take that back to the office for future study. And keep your eye out for a receipt, a piece of label, an empty bottle—anything that might relate to a prescription drug called digitalis."

"What for?"

Finn explained about Viola Beamer's overheard conversation, adding, "Don't forget to look inside every wadded-up bag."

"Right. Lesson Three again."

As they proceeded through the trash, one corner of the garage filled up with several charge slips, a paycheck stub, a paid phone bill, a handful of automated teller receipts, and two or three crumpled lottery tickets. Finn was disappointed at not finding any personal cards or letters to Viola Beamer, but he knew that what he had could be revealing—for both murder cases—upon further analysis.

Davis held up a can of Bud Light on a stick. "Think she was watchin' her weight?"

"Apparently she kept trim. I suppose that was important to her scam." A look around the garage told Finn there were fewer than ten Bud Light cans in the trash, not a lot for a hot summer week. Not even enough to produce a beer belly. If she were entertaining anybody on a regular basis they were both mild beer drinkers, or one didn't drink it at all. Finn also noted, almost without thinking, that there weren't any discarded booze bottles or matchbooks with the names of bars on them.

No crunched-up cigarette packages, either. *What a clean liver you were, you little murderess.*

Viola Beamer's reading matter, judging by her throw-aways, consisted of *TV Guide*, *Cosmopolitan*, *The National Enquirer*, and *Playgirl*. No *Good Housekeeping*.

"Hey," Davis said, "this chick's been playin' around." He held up an opened Trojan condom wrapper in his gloved fingers.

"Only one?" Finn asked.

"I think that's the box over there. But seriously, man, at her age?"

"'Sold only for the prevention of disease,' I believe the wrapper says."

Viola had been keeping company with a man, then. A lover, as Kendrake suggested early on. Finn doubted that the relationship started only after her latest husband's death. In fact, something told him it hadn't. Something he'd seen or heard…

Next to Davis's foot Finn spotted an empty prescription bottle. He pounced, picked it up. The label on the front, Finn noted with disappointment, indicated that it had held valium.

"Hey, Mr. Finn." Davis held up a canister. "Found somethin' wicked jammed down in a cereal box. Skull and crossbones right on the can."

Finn grabbed it. The bold letters above the familiar symbol for poison said ARSENIC. Smoot wasn't lying after all. Finn would have to destroy that incriminating videotape at the earliest opportunity. It boggled the mind.

"What do people use that shit for?" Davis asked.

"Industrial applications. Also, if I recall correctly, tanning, taxidermy, killing pests."

"And husbands."

"Not in this case. Digitalis was Mrs. Beamer's murder weapon, not arsenic."

"Oh, yeah? Arsenic is what we got here and it came from the lady's house. With her husband cremated, nobody can say that ain't what killed him."

Davis had that right. Or so Finn assumed. Although arsenic could be detected in hair and fingernails, Finn didn't think it would be found in ashes. If not, then arsenic poisoning couldn't be disproved using what was left of Otto Beamer. On the contrary, the canister in Finn's hand could be the foundation of a strong circumstantial case for murder.

And that, Finn realized, was the last thing he wanted at this point. Making a case against Mrs. Beamer would only strengthen the one against her stepson for murder, presuming the revenge motive. There was a definite crime to avenge now, not just a possible one. A prosecutor like Finn's pal Ernie Bittenbauer could go far with that.

Thanks to Davis, Finn was within a stone's throw of installing Norris Beamer as his father's heir and insurance beneficiary. But the only way to do it was to expose him to a greater likelihood of a murder conviction.

"Mr. Finn?"

"I'm thinking."

Red Dog McCorkle believed he could instill in the jury a reasonable doubt of Beamer's guilt by hammering on the presence of a black man on the murder night. But Finn knew that man was the innocent Shadd Davis. If the police tracked him down, Davis would be in trouble—especially since township police records would show he was picked up in Viola's neighborhood the week before. Finn might be able to rescue him by telling the whole story, but then Beamer's main defense would collapse. Either Finn's student would suffer, or his client—and neither deserved it.

Finn had a thumping headache. But through the pain it seemed clear to him that the best possible development, at least for now, would be for the mysterious black man to stay mysterious. That way his involvement could be neither proved nor disproved, either of which would be a blow to the A-Plus Detective Agency & Famous Detectives School.

"Mr. Davis," he said, "have you ever thought of applying your musical genius on the streets of, say, downtown Columbus or Louisville?"

He shook his head. "Couldn't leave town, Mr. Finn. Got my eye on this woman, see."

"I understand your reluctance, but I'm sure Brenda would still be around when you came back. I think a temporary absence would be in your best interests. A neighbor saw you outside of Mrs. Beamer's home last night shortly before her body was found."

"You shittin' me?"

"In view of your previous encounter with police on that same street—"

"*Damn.* I'll get packing."

"And take your brother's truck." Finn allowed himself a smile. That little maneuver should muck things up enough to buy him some time to work on Sheila LaFeulle and to produce other suspects. He wouldn't tell Beamer what he had done, or even Red Dog. The attorney would be all the more persuasive with his scenario of a burglar if he believed it himself.

The worst part of all this, even worse than losing Davis as a student, was knowing that Hawley Smoot had lived up to his side of the bargain.

Because that meant that Finn would have to honor his side, too.

TWENTY-TWO

COMING CLEAN

Sheila Graf LaFeulle lived in a high-rise apartment building overlooking the Ohio River. Also a high-rent apartment, Mobarry thought as he ascended the elevator to the nineteenth floor. Why would somebody who lived here be involved with Viola Beamer or her murder?

For that matter, why was *he* involved?

It was the kind of question his wife asked whenever he left the house at some weird hour or, like today, ducked out of work at Annie's Catering. It was her company, named after her by her father when he'd started it thirty-seven years ago. Except for sampling their wares, Mobarry had little interest in the business. He'd be happy spending his days with the scanners, tuning in on private lives and private lies. "Sick," Annie called it, but look where his hobby, indirectly, had gotten him now: on his way to interview a woman he himself had identified as a suspect.

Down the hallway and around the bend from the elevator, Mobarry rang the doorbell of Sheila LaFeulle's apartment. He had an Annie's Catering box in his hand and a microcassette recorder in his pocket.

On the third ring a woman in her mid- to late-forties opened the door and stuck her head out above the chain. She had sandy hair, cropped short and combed back from a face marked by a firm jawline that Mobarry found attractive. Round glasses. No makeup or jewelry.

"Yes?"

"Sheila LaFeulle?"

"There must be some mistake. I didn't order anything from a caterer."

He set down the box which, along with the Annie's Catering cap on his head, got him past the concierge. As he straightened up he slipped a hand in his pocket and clicked on the recorder.

"It's about Viola Beamer."

"What? I don't understand. Anyway, she's dead. I heard it on the radio."

"That's what I want to talk to you about."

The door slammed shut. When Mobarry realized she wasn't taking the chain off, he said in a loud voice, "I saw you outside her house this morning."

Sheila LaFeulle jerked open the door. "Who the hell are you?"

"The A-Plus Detective Agency. I'm incognito."

She moved to close the door again but Mobarry wedged his foot in the way. "We're working for Norris Beamer," he said. "You tried calling him a couple of days ago."

"I'm going to call the police if you don't get out of here."

Mobarry snorted. "You didn't seem too eager to talk to the cops this morning when you drove away from the Beamer house."

"What do you want?"

"Just to ask a few questions. I'll be in and out in twenty minutes."

"I don't let strangers in."

"Fine. Let's do it in the hallway, give the neighbors a treat." Finn would like that line, Mobarry thought.

"Oh, damn. Move your foot and I'll take the chain off."

"Promise?"

She promised.

When she opened the door, Mobarry saw that she was wearing pleated trousers, khaki, with a striped cotton shirt, ivory and cobalt blue. Her collar was buttoned down. She was about an inch shorter than his six feet.

"My name is Dick Mobarry."

She ignored his outstretched hand. "Let's just get on with this."

She turned off the television and sat at one end of a long couch next to a picture window with a river view, her legs crossed.

"Okay." Mobarry sat in a chair opposite. "What were you doing in front of Viola Beamer's house today? And don't say you were just driving by—your car was parked a few doors away on Wednesday."

"It's very simple." Sheila LaFeulle lit a cigarette. "Wednesdays and Fridays are the days I work for Viola Beamer. I'm her cleaning lady."

"That's crap."

She shook her head. "It is not."

"Cleaning ladies don't live in places like this."

"This one does." She exhaled smoke. "Look, I stayed home and raised Jack LaFeulle's kids for twenty-three years, then he dumped me for one of his vice presidents when he got to the top of the company. She's younger than our oldest daughter. I thought taking this job would embarrass him with his corporate peers—his ex-wife a cleaning lady. It was a lark."

Viola Beamer's words through his speakerphone came back to Mobarry: "Sheila! What the hell are you doing here? Don't you ever come in my house when I'm not here. My bedroom drawers were messed up after the last time you were here. And I've had that feeling before."

Mobarry had forgotten that until now, hadn't even mentioned it to Finn after the excitement of picking up the cellular call.

"You had an argument with Mrs. Beamer the day before she was killed," he said.

"How do you know that?"

He ignored the question. "She thought you were snooping around."

"Paranoia on her part. Guilty conscience."

"Guilty about what?"

Sheila LaFeulle crushed her cigarette in a crystal ash tray. "I think she killed her husband."

"Is that why you called Beamer?"

"Right. To tell him. Apparently, he already knew. Don't the police say that's why he killed her?"

"We think they're wrong. What made you suspicious about Otto Beamer's death?"

She shook her head. "It wouldn't do any good to talk about that now. Mrs. Beamer's dead and I don't want anything to do with it."

"Is that why you kept driving when you saw the sheriff's cars this morning?"

"Yes."

"It won't be that easy to stay out of this, Mrs. LaFeulle. The cops are probably going to talk to you at some point just because you were in her house a couple of days a week. They'll want to know what you know."

"Oh, hell. It's not that much." She lit another cigarette. "I caught signs here and there that she was entertaining a boyfriend. Then she'd call him sometimes and talk in a low voice. And I only started working for her after her husband was dead. Why would she be so sneaky about it if she hadn't started the affair while the old man was still alive?"

"That didn't mean she killed him."

"I didn't say I could prove it. But neighbors were practically tripping over themselves to tell me how healthy he was. A cold fish like her wouldn't blink at taking care of that."

"Maybe you read too many mysteries," Mobarry said. "I prefer biographies. Viola Beamer was a Lucrezia Borgia type if there ever was one. Do you have any idea why a money-grubbing bitch like that would spend money on cleaning help?"

"She lived like a pig and she paid me in pocket change to pick her clothes off the floor," Sheila LaFeulle said through cigarette smoke. "I think she had enough of the domestic angel routine when her husband was alive. Wanted to pamper herself a little."

"Do you have any idea who might have killed her?"

"If it wasn't Norris Beamer?" She shook her head. "No idea. But I wish him luck."

TWENTY-THREE

WHODUNIT?

Finn set the videocassette on his desk and smashed its plastic casing into pieces, using a duck-shaped metal bookend as a hammer. He was cutting up the tape itself with scissors when Kendrake entered his office.

"Whatever are you doing, Mr. Finn?"

The detective winced. "Keeping a promise to Hawley Smoot. And saying goodbye to our fee from Cheviot Mutual. It's a long, ugly story."

"I'd love to hear it, but this may be more urgent."

She handed Finn a registered letter from his landlord, Herman Schaeperklaus. Noting that the rent was two months overdue and that Finn's promised check bounced, Schaeperklaus threatened to start eviction proceedings unless Finn came up with real money within three business days.

"I was hoping to cover that check with the payment from Cheviot Mutual and cash flow from the correspondence school," Finn said. "Did any money come in today?"

"No."

Finn crumpled the letter and threw it in his wastebasket. Three business days—until Tuesday, then. Thank God his dad couldn't see him now.

"Don't worry about your salary, Mrs. Kendrake. I borrowed money from my mother to cover that."

"That wasn't a concern; I would get paid by Office Temps anyway." Kendrake's voice rose. "But I have to say I am disturbed that you let me go on about buying a computer when you can't even pay the rent."

"I didn't want to depress you with the facts."

"Then how can I possibly help you?" Kendrake took a deep breath. "Perhaps I can still negotiate with the landlord."

Finn shook his head. "I guarantee you he won't cut me any slack beyond what the law requires. I made the mistake of doing some investigative work in a negligence suit involving another property he owns. He would love to toss me out. Fortunately, we still have a little time. Eviction takes a while. If we can rack up enough hours working for Norris Beamer's murder defense—"

"There's a little problem with that," Kendrake said. "I took the liberty of investigating Beamer's credit rating, the way they did at that property management firm where I worked a couple of weeks ago. The man's a worse credit risk than you are. He owes everybody, including an ex-wife. That must be why he was so concerned about his inheritance. You're not going to get any money out of him."

"But we're working for Red Dog."

"If McCorkle doesn't receive his fee from Beamer, he'll drag his feet so long on paying us that we'll be evicted and maybe in bankruptcy court before we see any of his cash."

Finn repressed a strong urge to scream. "Do you see any way out, Mrs. Kendrake? Any way at all?"

She sat down. "Well, Beamer will have plenty of money if he inherits his father's. We just have to somehow prove both that his stepmother is disqualified from inheriting and that he isn't."

"That's going to be tougher than you think. I guess I'd better tell you a few things, and none of it is pretty."

He began by explaining his devil's bargain with Smoot, trying to ignore the disappointment in her eyes. He went on to tell her about Smoot finding the container of arsenic and the body, and about Davis recovering the poison from a trash bag.

"I just can't figure it." Finn unwrapped a cigar. "There could be a legitimate reason for an individual to have arsenic in the house, but no multiple murderer would leave it lying around even though it isn't the murder weapon. 'The guilty flee where no man pursueth.' I couldn't wait to get that canister into my safe deposit box—and I have a clean conscience, at least by comparison. In short, this has all the fragrance of a setup. But who? And why?"

"Can't a buyer of poison be traced?" Kendrake asked.

"Easily—in detective novels."

"Forgive me for changing the subject, Mr. Finn, but I keep wondering who killed Viola."

Finn lit his smoke. "Well, Dick Mobarry's drive-by suspect seems a good possibility. We'll know better when we get his report on her. Otherwise, lovers and partners in crime are always strong suspects—and Viola appears to have had both, presumably the same person."

"But why would her partner kill her? She's the key operator—the one who married the elderly gentlemen. Getting rid of her would be a classic case of killing the goose that laid the golden egg."

"Maybe it was a crime of passion." Finn repressed a shudder. He had a mental image of Viola Beamer as a huge spider with dyed brown hair. "Maybe her lover and her partner were not the same and the two had a conflict. At any rate, there was a lover."

"And it's more important than ever to find out who."

Finn eyed Kendrake. "Are you finally going tell me you went behind my back and got Chandler to check into those two male neighbors?"

She took a deep breath. "I was just doing what I thought you'd do if you weren't so distracted with other problems, Mr. Finn. How did you know?"

Finn held up two sheets of notes. "She phoned in her findings earlier, while you were out shopping."

"Anything significant?"

"You want to be the detective—you tell me how significant it is." He passed the notes to Kendrake.

"Bessie Longdale's son is a womanizer, and Viola was a woman," she said after studying the data. "So that fits. It also looks like he's paying heavily for his divorce, so he could use money. And he did have the opportunity to know Viola, since his mother lived across the street."

"Okay, so he can't be ruled out, but there's not a lot to rule him in. He's a maybe. How about Hackleshin?"

"That one has a monetary motive for being involved with Viola, if not a romantic one. Maybe he's not anybody's idea of a lover, but he could be a partner. Then both of these men could have been involved with her."

Finn re-lit his dead cigar. "Why would Viola need Hackleshin? A woman like that isn't going to cut somebody in on the action unless he's a lust-interest or unless he fulfills some other necessary function. Any ideas?"

"Just that I think you ought to take another look at Mr. F.'s report." She plucked a manila file folder from the stack on Finn's desk and handed it to him.

"Why?" he asked.

"Maybe something in it will take on a new meaning now that we know a lot more about all the people on that street, including Viola Bcamer."

"Worth a try, I suppose." Finn spoke without enthusiasm. But after several minutes of study, he thumped the desk. "I don't believe it—there *is* something!"

"What?"

"A contradiction, I think. Funderburgh quotes the woman across the street as saying Viola had a son who only visited her when her husband was away."

"And?"

Finn paged through the fattest folder on his desk. "Just as I remembered. Chandler's research indicates that Viola didn't have any children. Unless she had a secret offspring somewhere along the line, that was no son the neighbor met; it was probably the boyfriend. Unfortunately, there's no description of him in the report. We need to get Funderburgh back into the neighborhood to find out more about this occasional visitor."

Kendrake stood. "I'll get him on the phone."

But she returned a moment later from her desk, where she kept all the students' phone numbers. "No answer. Should we dispatch another student?"

"Who, for example?"

"How about Joe Canova?"

Mike Hammer with arrogance, Finn thought. "Any other suggestions?"

"Mary Sue Barkeloo?"

Spiky hair and bubble gum.

"Try Funderburgh again later." And yet, Finn felt a twinge of conscience. He should find something for Barkeloo to do, something that she couldn't screw up. A challenge, that. "Meanwhile—"

Finn bent over, picked up a cardboard box from the floor and set it on the top of the desk. "This is the paperwork Shadd Davis and I set aside from Viola's trash. There might well be something revealing in here."

"Like a love letter?"

They had no such luck. But every item in the box told Finn something about Viola Beamer. The discarded lottery tickets showed she was interested in money and was a bit of a gambler, but of course Finn already knew that. The three unopened envelopes from financial institutions proffering unsolicited loans demonstrated she was a good credit risk—again, no surprise. The figure on the paycheck stub was modest, but then Viola had other substantial income. She bought her underwear at Kmart and her groceries at Thriftway. She never took more than thirty dollars at a time from a Jeanie automated teller machine. The phone bills from Cincinnati Bell and CelTel, the cellular phone company, showed one telephone in the house, one in the car, and no long distance calls.

"The woman was tight with a dollar," Kendrake said. "How come she spent the money for a car phone?"

"Probably because she made a lot of calls she didn't want her husband to hear, and her husband was almost always around the house."

Amanda, who had been reading another comic book at the reception desk, stuck her head in the door. "There's somebody to see you."

Close behind her was a smiling Dick Mobarry. "Hi, Mr. Finn, Mrs. Kendrake."

Finn rose. "I hope you're bringing us a report on Sheila La-Feulle, Mr. Mobarry."

"Something better—a tape." He held up a microrecorder. "I carried this on me so you could hear the interview yourself."

"Excellent idea."

Mobarry set the recorder on Finn's desk and played the tape. As he turned it off, Finn said:

"That argument with Viola could have been a lot more significant than she let on. You should have told me about that before."

"Sorry."

"She could have stolen something valuable and killed to cover it up when Viola got suspicious. Viola could have afforded to have something valuable."

"LaFeulle is apparently well off, too," Kendrake pointed out. "Suppose she got that way by stealing from other clients, not from a divorce settlement?"

"We can check on that through the divorce records at the Court House. If she's a thief and a killer, why would she bother to call Beamer and tell him his father may have been murdered?"

Mobarry beat Finn with an answer: "Maybe she was hoping he'd be so pissed he'd take care of his stepmother and she wouldn't have to."

Finn shook his head. "That's a bit thin, I'm afraid."

Mobarry shrugged. "Well, anyway, I have something else for you."

He pulled a piece of paper from the breast pocket of his wrinkled shirt. "I should have brought you this a couple of days ago, only I forgot. Before I slipped that bug into Mrs. Beamer's phone she was talking to somebody on it. When I left she wrote down his name and the phone number on a little notepad by the phone. Thought it might be important, so I took the second sheet off the pad. It was still in my shirt when I pre-sorted the laundry last night."

Mobarry handed the paper to Finn. "I figured you could rub a pencil over it and bring out the writing from the top sheet on the pad."

"Just like Nancy Drew," Amanda commented from the doorway.

"Back to your desk, young lady," her mother ordered as Finn scowled.

How is it her *desk?* he thought.

The girl disappeared.

Never in twenty-five years of law enforcement work had Finn seen the old impression-on-a-pad-of-paper dodge worked in real life, but he wasn't about to discourage initiative in a student. Without comment, he applied the edge of a pencil point to the paper. The name "Doug" and a seven-digit number emerged in white.

"Mr. Mobarry," Finn said, "this could be of immense importance in clearing our client of a murder charge. Once again you have done well."

Mobarry left a few minutes later with a grin on his face, no doubt convinced that he was the star of the case.

He had barely cleared the doorway before Finn pulled the *Williams City Directory*, a reverse-lookup directory, from his bottom drawer. "Do you think this Doug is Viola's boyfriend?" Kendrake asked.

"I think it's certainly possible."

Finn ran his finger down the columns of phone numbers until he found the one matching the paper in his other hand. "It's a downtown business. 'Intimate Images.' Let's have one of our sleuths check it out. We'll find out what Doug looks like and compare him to whatever description we can get of Viola's 'son.'"

Kendrake already had the phone to her ear. "How about Chandler? She works downtown."

Finn shook his head. "She refuses to do interviews."

"Let me ask her."

Finn left the room while Kendrake made the call. It would be embarrassing to hear her beg to no avail, even though he thought it might do her good to be cut down a notch or two.

He came back in five minutes, just in time to hear Kendrake say, "Thanks, Rosalee."

"For nothing?" he asked after she hung up.

"She's on her way out of town for a library seminar this weekend."

"Is she?" Finn tried not to smile.

"But she'll talk to Doug on Monday."

"What? How did you get her to agree to that?"

"I appealed to her woman to woman."

"Oh."

It would sound like sour grapes to say that Monday was a long time to wait, even though it was.

"She's going to check the LaFeulle divorce records, too," Kendrake added.

Without a word, Finn rummaged through the box on his desk. He stopped when he came to Viola Beamer's phone bills. "Telephone records! That's how we can find out without question who Viola called that morning Mobarry was listening in. I'm an idiot for not thinking of that before."

"I thought there were only records of long distance calls."

"Cellular phones are billed by the call, so there must be a record of every call. These bills are for last month, but surely a customer can inquire what calls he's placed since the last bill?"

"But you aren't the customer."

"CelTel won't know that. The phone bills are in the name of a man, Otto Beamer, although I'm sure he never saw them."

Kendrake shook her head. "You don't mind lying at all, do you?"

"Sleuths don't lie. We use pretexts. Pay attention now." Finn picked up the telephone.

He started with the business office phone number on page one of the CelTel bill. He was switched only twice and put on hold once, for thirty-four seconds, before he reached the appropriate person.

"Yes, I can send you a listing of your calls," that person said.

"You don't understand, ma'am." Finn let panic creep into his voice. "This is important. It could be life or death." Kendrake, sitting in one of the chairs, folded her arms and looked at him. He turned away so he couldn't see her. "It's my little girl. She's run away from home. I'm sure she must have told some friends what she was going to do. She hangs on the phone by the hour, even in the car—but I don't know who her friends are. If I can find them, maybe they'll talk. I can't wait days. Susie could be in Orlando or Tampa by then."

"I understand, sir. I have a daughter of my own. She once— But I can't give out customer information over the phone."

"I'm the customer! Don't you believe me? Here's my account number." He read it off.

"Just a minute, sir." Finn heard a sigh, then buttons being punched on the computer console. "Can you write this down?"

Finn already had his pen poised over a yellow legal pad. "I'm ready."

It took only a few minutes to get it all.

"You'll never know what this means to me," Finn told the CelTel employee.

"I think I do."

No, you don't, he thought as he hung up.

"That was heart-wrenching," Kendrake said acidly. "You were almost crying."

"I just imagined losing our fee because Red Dog drained all of Norris Beamer's disposable funds before we got our share," Finn fibbed. In truth he was remembering how he once used the same technique to help a friend find his runaway daughter. Now the girl had a husband and a daughter of her own—Finn's goddaughter. How the years flew by.

Kendrake bent over Finn's shoulder to look at the list of Viola's cellular calls over the last two weeks of her life, with the date and time of each call.

"But this doesn't show a call Thursday morning," Kendrake said. "How can that be? Mobarry heard it."

The smell of her perfume enveloped Finn and made it hard to concentrate. He forced himself to think business.

"There was a call, but we've only been assuming Viola made it. Maybe her lover called her."

"Then all these numbers are useless."

"Maybe not. Let's see who she called."

They looked up each phone number in the *Williams City Directory*. The Eternal Rest Funeral Home had been called several times, the directory showed. So had Corwin Liggett and the Hanging Gardens. Intimate Images had been called once.

"Do you know Liggett?" Finn asked.

Kendrake looked over at him from the directory. "Just by reputation."

"It's all true."

Liggett was a lawyer, and a bad one. Finn had only once laid eyes on him, enough to note that he bore an amazing resemblance to a light bulb with legs. But Liggett was a legend in the prosecutor's office and in the press room. Consensus had it that he couldn't find the Court House without directions hidden in one of his four-inch-wide ties. Many thought he passed the bar exam the same way, while others attached significance to the fact that his mother was a federal judge. His defenders argued that his fees were modest and his clients got what they paid for.

"This last number is Bessie Longdale's," Kendrake reported. "Which means it's also Bessie Longdale's son's. It was called twice."

Finn shrugged. "Longdale could hardly be the man introduced to his own mother as Viola's son. Besides, both calls were after

Beamer was dead. That doesn't do much to show a murder conspiracy. This whole list is disappointing. Viola called the funeral home that handled her husband's body, she called her lawyer, she called a neighbor, and she called her employer. Nothing suspicious about any of that."

"Are you sure?"

"Hmmm. Well, maybe we should pay more attention to the Hanging Gardens Retirement Center. Work places are often scenes of romance. And tension. I wish our inside agent was still there."

"Mrs. Pertwee? She is."

Finn stared. "She didn't check out after the news of Viola's murder?"

Kendrake shook her head. "Amanda took a message while you and I were out earlier. Mrs. Pertwee phoned and asked you to call her at the nursing home."

"Why didn't you tell me before?"

"Amanda didn't remember until about an hour ago. I came in here to tell you, but we started talking about Hawley Smoot and I got off track. I'm sorry."

The detective glanced at his watch. Six o'clock. "There must not be any urgency by now. I think I'll stop by tomorrow—I'd like to look over the Hanging Gardens myself anyway. Would you please try Funderburgh again before we leave for the day?"

But he could not be reached.

TWENTY-FOUR

CAR WASH

Joe Canova, dressed in his Saturday best T-shirt and cutoff jeans, rubbed and buffed and polished until his red Mustang shone in the sunlight on his driveway.

Then he polished again, thinking about the phone call he'd received from Finn that morning. The little shit had come crawling, wanting him to talk to the dead Viola's neighbors and find out everything he could about a man who'd been presented as her son.

Finn had given him the name of one nosy woman in particular—Bessie Longdale, who lived across the street. She was one of the ones that old guy in the class, Funderburgh, had talked to before, Finn said. So why hadn't Finn sent him back there?

Because cream rises to the top, Canova answered himself as he wiped beads of water off an outside mirror. His videotape proved to Finn that he had the right stuff. If that snooty Chandler hadn't been so full of her own show-and-tell she would have been impressed, too. She'd hardly looked at him during class. Envious, maybe? Sometimes it didn't pay to show up a woman. Maybe that had been his problem with Sheri, his most recent ex-girlfriend.

Canova sat behind the wheel to wash his inside windshield. As soon as he finished he'd go to the car show at the Convention Center, and tomorrow he had to work at the fire house. So it would be Monday before he could do the detective routine in Viola Beamer's neighborhood. He hadn't bothered to tell Finn that. V.B. was dead and she wouldn't be any deader by Monday, right? Canova stretched to reach the far end of the windshield with his cloth.

"Hello, Joe."

Mary Sue Barkeloo stood on his driveway, decked out in a well-filled yellow halter top and plaid capri pants. Canova was so surprised that he jerked to the left, somehow hitting the horn and producing a brief but nerve-jangling burst of sound. Flustered, he jumped out of the car. Even in flipflops, Barkeloo towered over him.

"You're not going to slap me again are you?" he asked, remembering their aborted date.

"Don't be silly. A girl can't blame a guy for trying. I'm here to help." She looked serious. She wasn't even blowing bubbles.

I must be dreaming, Canova thought. *And I don't want to wake up.*

"Well, that's nice. I just finished, but you could help me down a few drinks at the Blue Lagoon around the corner."

"I want to help on a case, I mean. Be your assistant, like. Mr. Finn never asks me to do anything."

"You look cute when you pout."

Apparently, that was the wrong thing to say.

"You bastard." Barkeloo hauled back her right hand. Prepared this time, Canova lifted his own to block. But they were both startled by a third voice.

"Mr. Canova?"

"Now what?"

"I'm sorry. I didn't mean to interrupt."

Canova saw the beard first. To him, all bearded men looked more or less the same. This one happened to be wearing tan slacks and a polo shirt. It took Canova a moment to place him.

"You're that mummy guy," he said. "The undertaker."

"Funeral director," Greylock corrected.

"Whatever. How'd you find me? My business card doesn't have an address."

"The phone book does. You're the only Joseph Canova listed. I hope you don't mind my stopping by. I've been thinking about the allegations against Mrs. Beamer since our talk the other day. Then when I heard she was murdered... Well, I couldn't help but wonder if you found out anything."

"Meet my, uh, assistant, Ms. Barkeloo." While they shook hands, Canova lit a cigarette. "What's your interest?"

"I knew Mrs. Beamer, however briefly. In fact, I'm in charge of her arrangements. If what you said about her husband being murdered is true, and if it gets out, our establishment could become connected in the public mind with that sort of thing. The connotation would be most unpleasant."

Unlike death by cancer or car wreck, I suppose, Canova thought.

"So it would greatly relieve my mind to know that this is all going to be resolved quickly," Greylock concluded. "Both deaths, hopefully."

Ghoulish busybody. Canova shook his head. "I can't talk about my investigation. That wouldn't be ethical."

"I saw on the news that Mrs. Beamer's stepson was arrested. He's the one who suspected her of killing his father, isn't he?"

Canova dropped his cigarette on the driveway and crushed it with a sandaled foot. "I like to ask the questions, Bub. Like for instance, did you ever see Viola Beamer being squired around by a younger man?"

Greylock rubbed his bearded chin. "How much younger?"

"Young enough that people believed he was her son."

"Oh, yes, I remember now. He was with her the first time she came in. They seemed unusually affectionate."

"I'll bet." This was manna from heaven. "What was his name?"

"She didn't introduce him."

"What did she call him when she talked to him?" Barkeloo asked. *Good question*, Canova thought, surprised.

Greylock shrugged. "'Honey' or 'dear'—something like that."

"What did he look like?"

"I couldn't say. I gave the widow my fullest attention."

"She wasn't *that* hot. You must remember something about her son. What color was his hair?"

Greylock thought a moment. "It was light. Red or blond, I think."

"Did he have a mustache?"

"No, no facial hair."

"How old was he?"

"In his late twenties, I would guess."

"Tall?"

"Perhaps half a foot shorter than me." About five-seven, then.

"Handsome?" Barkeloo asked.

"I really didn't notice."

After he left, Canova said, "See how it's done? I got a description of the boyfriend and I haven't even talked to the neighbors yet."

"Is that your next move?"

"That's my assignment."

"I'm going with you."

* * * * *

On the way to his car, Bill Longdale looked across the street at the yellow CRIME SCENE tape in front of the Beamer house. No way would he go near the house as long as that stuff was up. That was asking for trouble.

But when it came down, he had to get back in there.

TWENTY-FIVE

REST HOME

Finn called Kendrake on Saturday afternoon.

"Sorry to bother you on an off day," he said, "but I thought you'd want to know that Mr. Funderburgh never answered his phone. I finally stooped to putting Canova on the job."

Even over the phone lines she sounded concerned. "Do you think something's wrong with him? He does live alone. Anything could have happened."

"I intend to stop by his house after I visit Mrs. Pertwee at the retirement center."

"I'd like to go with you. Both places."

The prospect of company was welcome, but Finn didn't want to ruin Kendrake's Saturday. "You don't have to do that."

"I'm interested. Besides, Amanda went to Kings Island with a friend and her family and I have nothing better to do. You won't even have to pay me."

Sold!

Half an hour later Finn picked Kendrake up in his Ohio-made Honda. She brought flowers for Mrs. Pertwee.

"Red Dog called me earlier this afternoon," Finn said as he pulled away from her house. "He wanted to know how we're doing at finding his burglar."

"How are we doing?"

"Splendid. We have his name already, but he's left town. We'll stay on it until we find him. Red Dog was impressed. He got our mutual client out on bail, by the way. The other news hasn't been so good. The coroner says Viola died of gunshots above her left ear and above her left eye between 3 P.M. and 9 P.M. on Thursday. Beamer has an alibi for the first couple of hours of that—he was at work—but not the rest."

"I bet that timing has McCorkle confused." Kendrake watched the speedometer needle with obvious apprehension. "*I'm* confused, and I know a lot more about what happened that night than he does."

Finn nodded. "He's still hanging on to his burglar-as-killer theory, though. The argument would be that the killer stayed in the house with the body for hours after the murder. Or Red Dog could find a forensic pathologist somewhere, one of those professional witnesses, to impeach the coroner's finding on the time of death."

"If that's his best shot, Norris Beamer is lucky the case against him is so circumstantial. Could you please slow down a little, Mr. Finn? My daughter has expensive tastes and I'm not that well insured."

Finn eased up on the gas pedal. "Unfortunately, Red Dog said that circumstantial evidence has gotten stronger. One of Beamer's co-workers at the savings and loan told the police Beamer was deeply upset about being disinherited by his father. Apparently, he talked about it several times, and made it clear that he blamed his stepmother. That supports the revenge motive."

"Not good."

"It gets worse. Beamer's ex-wife, a scorned woman, called the police and told them he owns a handgun. Beamer admitted it to Red Dog, but said he recently lost the weapon."

"How convenient. Did you ever consider that maybe Beamer did kill Viola?"

Finn shook his head. "The way I read him, I still don't buy revenge. I'm just afraid a jury might."

"Then let's hope this never gets to a jury," Kendrake said.

Finn tightened his hands on the steering wheel. "We're going to find the killer before it comes to that. We just have to."

He swung the car into the parking lot of the Hanging Gardens Retirement Center. "With Canova going to Viola's neighborhood, Chandler at Intimate Images, and Mrs. Pertwee here, something has to break soon."

Finn had never been in a retirement home. His first impression of the Hanging Gardens was institutional squalor: tile floor, dim light, handrails on the walls, the faint stench of urine. Vacant eyes stared at Finn from slack-jawed residents in wheel chairs clustered just inside the doorway, the anteroom of purgatory. A frail man with a fringe of white hair around his spotted skull listed to one side in his chair, his mouth hanging open. A woman young enough to be the old man's great-granddaughter stuck a cigarette into a holder, and the holder into his mouth. She lit the cigarette for him. He made an appreciative grunt. Finn thought that he would never again be afraid of dying.

He told the faded red-head at the reception desk that they were there to visit Mrs. Pertwee.

"She'll be so happy to see you," the nursing home employee said in the same loud voice and slightly patronizing tone she probably used on the center's residents all day long.

She directed them to room 36 down the hall.

"I wish we hadn't done this to Mrs. Pertwee," Finn said in a low voice as they walked in that direction.

They found her sitting up in a chair. She had a visitor in the chair next to her, holding her hand. The sight of him took Finn's breath away.

"Mr. Funderburgh!"

That gentleman turned pale. "Er, hello there." He quickly withdrew his hand from Mrs. Pertwee's.

So this was why Funderburgh hadn't been home to answer his phone! Years of studying ten new vocabulary words a day hadn't equipped Finn to verbalize his emotions. He stood mute.

Kendrake put the flowers on the night stand. "Thank you, dear," Mrs. Pertwee said in her high-pitched voice. "So thoughtful of you two to visit."

"We didn't come to give you company," Finn said in a strangled voice. "And you don't appear to be needing any."

Funderburgh stood up. "I suppose I should explain what I'm doing here. When I appeared at Krohn Conservatory yesterday morning to meet the SWF who answered my ad, I fully expected to see Viola Beamer. I didn't know she was dead then. Imagine my surprise when the woman with the orchid turned out to be Mrs. Pertwee!"

Mrs. Pertwee dimpled. Finn felt an urge to strangle her. "I've been answering 'personals' for years," she said.

"The ad specified a woman fifty to sixty years old," Finn pointed out. "You aren't—oh, never mind."

He threw up his hands in disgust.

"We assumed the letter was from Viola Beamer because the envelope had 'Hanging Gardens Retirement Center' printed on it," Kendrake said. "But I suppose the residents are issued stationery?"

Mrs. Pertwee nodded. "One of the few extravagances in this dreary place."

Finn looked around, silently counting to ten in a Herculean effort to control his fury. The room had flower-print curtains, lamps that needed new shades, and a color TV so old it had been made in America. It wasn't the room Finn would choose to die in, but then most people who came here didn't have a choice. This was a place for people who had no place else to go, people who were neither on welfare nor clipping coupons. The same kind of people, Finn realized with a start, who in a different stage of life could count on the A-Plus Detective Agency to handle their investigative needs.

"How is it here?" he asked Mrs. Pertwee.

"Wretched. This place reeks of despair."

"I thought it was Lysol and urine. Why did you call me yesterday?"

"When I heard that Viola Beamer had been murdered, I thought you'd want to know she had an argument the night before she died with Mr. Chavez, the administrator here. I was listening outside his office door during the fracas, but I couldn't hear much. I had the impression he was threatening her, though."

Finn looked at Kendrake with triumph in his eye. "Now we're getting somewhere."

"Not that I think he had anything to do with the murder," Mrs. Pertwee said. "Mr. Chavez is such a nice man, and he does the best he can. I'm sure it's not his fault if a staff member gets herself murdered and a resident disappears all within a few days."

"Disappears?" Finn and Kendrake said at once.

Mrs. Pertwee primped her white hair. "She wandered away, most likely. It happened Monday."

"Quite a coincidence," Kendrake said. "Two exciting occurrences in the same week."

"And you know what I said about coincidences in Lesson Three, Mrs. Pertwee," Finn added. "Always mistrust them." Deciding that Kendrake was officially off-duty in her secretarial role, he pulled out a pocket notebook and a pen. "Tell us about the person who disappeared."

"Her name was Virginia Hartwell and she was a pest. Nobody's sorry to see her go. She was always butting into games, offering her opinions where they weren't wanted, snooping around in other peoples' business."

"Where did you hear that?" Kendrake asked.

"From Mrs. Beamer. She liked to gossip."

That sounded promising to Finn. "If this Hartwell ever turns up, I'd like to talk to her. Or maybe we could help make her turn up. I'm going to have a chat with that nice Mr. Chavez."

Kendrake stayed with the two geriatric students while Finn strolled down the hall. Passing an ancient woman making cat noises in a wheel chair, he went into a room marked with the plastic nameplate "RICHARD CHAVEZ."

It was probably the most cheerful room at the retirement center, with live flowers in a vase, tasteful decorating in pastel colors, and a bookcase under the window sill. A man in his mid-fifties looked up from the computer on his desk when Finn entered. He had dark, wavy hair and a mustache.

"May I help you?" His voice oozed sincerity.

"I hope so." Making a snap decision, Finn handed him a business card with his real name and that of the A-Plus Detective Agency. No pretext this time.

"Private detective?" Chavez said, reading it. "What brings you here?"

"The murder of Viola Beamer."

Chavez shook his head. "A shocking crime. I still can't believe it."

"The A-Plus Detective Agency is acting on behalf of Mrs. Beamer's stepson, who has been arrested in connection with the crime. I'd like to ask you a few questions."

"I see." Chavez drummed the table with his fingers. "I'm sorry, Mr. Finn, but I don't want to get mixed up in a murder case in any way, shape, or form."

"I can understand that, but I'm trying to help defend an innocent man who didn't want to be involved in this affair either. Norris Beamer is a businessman, just like you. Two days ago, he was running a profitable savings and loan. Yesterday he was put in a holding cell. In a few months he could be doing time with an overly friendly roommate and bars on his windows."

Chavez fiddled with a paperweight—an American flag encased in plastic. "That has nothing to do with me."

Finn sat in the chair placed in front of Chavez's desk and leaned forward. "I'll tell you what has to do with you: You had an argument with Mrs. Beamer in this office the day before she died. Do you want to tell me about it?"

Chavez froze. "No, Mr. Finn, I don't. It was a disciplinary matter that couldn't possibly have anything to do with her murder."

"Are you sure it wasn't a more personal issue? Like a quarrel between lovers and partners?"

"What?" The administrator's jaw dropped.

"If you have a better explanation, you're either going to tell me or tell Norris's attorney on the witness stand."

Chavez shut his eyes. "I should've played golf today. All right, then, but I hope you'll keep this strictly confidential. It was an embarrassing thing to have happen here. I had to warn Mrs. Beamer her job was in jeopardy because a resident's medicine disappeared some weeks ago on her watch. It had just come to my attention."

"How did she react?"

"Loudly. She told me to watch what I said—implying a slander suit. She knew I couldn't prove she'd lost the digitalis, but I felt sure that she had. She protested too much."

Finn swallowed. "Digitalis? That was the missing medicine?"

Chavez nodded. "This time."

Digitalis stolen from the nursing home to kill Otto Beamer made a lot more sense than the arsenic in the kitchen had. Finn had enough evidence now to mount a convincing case against Viola Beamer in Otto's murder—probably as strong as one could get without a body or a confession. Finn was optimistic that Norris Beamer could claim the victim's insurance and the estate.

Staying out of jail to enjoy it would be another matter. For Finn had just established a 24-carat motive for Beamer killing his stepmother.

Finn stood up. "I'm sure you were right to begin with: This digitalis business has nothing to do with Viola's murder. Don't volunteer anything about it to the police. But don't forget it either, because I may ask you about it later."

Chavez blinked at Finn. "I don't understand."

"You will. One more thing before I go: I heard that one of your residents disappeared the other day."

"Who told you that?"

"A friend. I just want to say you might consider hiring the A-Plus Detective Agency to find this woman. Our rates are reasonable, and the service is good."

"We've notified her family, who live out of town, and filed a report with the police. I'm sure that will be sufficient. We are concerned, but not overly so. Miss Hartwell isn't the first resident to have wandered off from here."

"What did she look like?"

"Gray hair, about five-five. It's in the police report."

"Did she take any medication regularly? That's always important in finding a missing person."

"Just digitalis. She was the person whose medicine was missing."

TWENTY-SIX

REAL REVENGE?

"Mr. Funderburgh and Mrs. Pertwee make a cute couple, don't you think?" Kendrake asked.

Finn grunted, slumped in his chair with the dejected air of the loser in a heavyweight prize fight. He had spent the rest of Saturday and all of Sunday smoking and thinking, except for Mass on Sunday, during which he skipped the smoking. Last night he dreamed again that he and Kendrake were The Avengers, this time in an episode about spies who faked a series of deaths and planted radar-jamming devices in the coffins. Now it was Monday morning, his mouth felt like an ash tray, and he still didn't know who had killed Viola Beamer.

The gas and electric bill lay on his desk unopened, like a love letter from a scorned sweetheart. It represented one of Finn's less worrisome financial obligations.

He only had until tomorrow to come up with the rent money he owed Schaeperklaus or the gears of the eviction process would begin grinding this whole operation to a pulp.

Finn would miss running his own business. But maybe not as much as he would miss Kendrake.

"How do you think the disappearance of that woman from the nursing home fits in?" she asked.

Finn rallied. "Miss Hartwell was a notorious pest and snoop—or so Viola Beamer herself told Mrs. Pertwee. I suspect she saw something that connected the missing digitalis with the murder of Viola's husband, prompting Viola to do away with her. The part I still can't fathom is the arsenic in Viola's kitchen. Why would she leave it there?"

Kendrake shrugged. "By the way, Mrs. Pertwee called. She couldn't find anybody at the Hanging Gardens who thought Viola had something going with Richard Chavez."

It had never been much of a hope; just a possibility a good detective couldn't ignore.

"Any word from Chandler?" Finn asked.

"Not a peep."

"Or Canova?"

"Ditto."

It depressed Finn to be so dependent on a man like Canova. If only Funderburgh hadn't been at the nursing home dallying with Mrs. Pertwee when Finn had needed someone to visit Cherry Tree Lane...

"Couldn't we go back to Viola's cleaning lady?" Kendrake said. "She might know what that phony son looked like."

"Do you still have her phone number?"

Silly question. The Compleat Secretary went to her desk and brought back the note she had taken from Finn's cousin Bill at the BMV. On top of all the information from her driver's license it was headlined SHEILA GRAF LAFEULLE.

Finn stared. "I've seen that name before."

"LaFeulle?"

"Graf." He rooted through Chandler's file for the obituary notices until he found it:

> GRAF
> LeRoy W., loving husband of Viola (née Hunnicut), devoted father of Sheila Graf LaFeulle of Los Angeles, grandfather of Jason and Jennifer LaFeulle, brother of the late Charles and William Graf. June 28. Age 76. Member of St. Stephen's Catholic Order of the Foresters. Memorial Mass at St. Mary Magdalene Church, Monday, July 2 at 10 A.M. Visitation Sunday from 5-8 P.M. Sunday at the Eternal Rest Funeral Home, 1135 Schaefer Pike.

"But she didn't mention this to Dick Mobarry," Kendrake said.

"She may have had good reason. Her father was killed by Viola Beamer. We could be wrong about our whole approach to this case and the prosecutor could be right—about the revenge motive, at least. This calls for another chat with Sheila Graf LaFeulle."

"Whom should we send?"

Finn stood up. "I think it's time we send ourselves."

* * * * *

"Isn't that her car?" Kendrake said. A woman was getting out of a yellow Camaro in the parking lot of Sheila LaFeulle's building. "It matches the description."

Finn opened his car door and called "Ms. LaFeulle!" as he got out. She stopped and looked in his direction with a puzzled expression on her face. "Ms. LaFeulle?" he repeated as he and Kendrake got closer.

"Mrs. What do you want?"

He decided on a frontal assault with the truth.

"We're from the A-Plus Detective Agency—"

"Oh, no." She started to stalk away.

"—and we want to talk about your father."

Sheila LaFeulle stopped again. "What about my father?"

"He was murdered by his wife. Just like Norris Beamer's father."

"I know that." Sunlight glinted off her glasses.

"Is that why you killed Viola Beamer?"

Her mouth fell open. "Killed— That's absurd!"

"It doesn't seem so far-fetched to me. You're obviously a woman of means, yet you took a job as a cleaning lady for the woman who murdered your father. Why—if not to kill her?"

"I don't have to answer to you." She folded her arms over her chest. "And if you think you can get Beamer off the hook by making a case against me, forget it. I can prove I was here in this building the whole night she died. I ate dinner in the restaurant and worked out in the gym. People saw me."

Finn felt like he was being sucked down a whirlpool. "Then why didn't you tell my st— my detective that you were Viola Beamer's stepdaughter?"

"Why should I? That kind of connection got Norris Beamer arrested, didn't it?"

Finn ignored the question. "You admit knowing she killed your father. How did you know that? And why did you go to work for her? It wasn't to embarrass your ex-husband, the line you fed Dick Mobarry."

A car drove past. "You have to admit it's a little hard to understand," Kendrake said.

Sheila LaFeulle turned to her. "Maybe you can understand *this*. When your husband's dumped you for a younger woman and your kids have left you for college, you tend to dwell on the past. It got worse when I moved back to Cincinnati. I began remembering things of Mother's I wanted to have. I tried to establish contact with my stepmother to get them back—pay, if I had to—but I couldn't find her. So I hired Worldwide Investigations."

"And they gave you the news that she'd been married multiple times to elderly men," Finn guessed. "And her husbands had a habit of dying."

She nodded. "It was obvious that she was a fortune-hunter. I decided to watch her for a while and figure out a way to spoil her game. When I heard she was looking for a cleaning woman, it seemed perfect. I applied for the job, using some friends as references; they thought it was a joke."

"When did you determine she was a murderer?" Kendrake asked.

"I didn't 'determine' anything. It became clear as I learned more about her other husbands. They all seemed to have died unexpectedly. If you'll excuse me—"

Kendrake stepped in front of her. "Maybe we can help each other, Mrs. LaFeulle. Our agency was hired to prove that Viola Beamer was a murderer before it was hired to prove that her stepson isn't. We still hope to do that. If we succeed, you may be able to recover some damages from her estate. So it's in your best interests to help us."

Sheila LaFeulle opened her purse and pulled out a pack of cigarettes.

"What I lost to that woman I could never recover. And I don't need the money. I have plenty of that, thanks to my ex. But maybe some of the others— How could I help?"

"While you were working for her, did she ever have a visitor who claimed to be her son?" Finn asked.

She shook her head as she lit up.

"You told Mr. Mobarry you saw signs of a lover. Do you have any idea who he was—either a first or a last name?"

"I'm afraid not."

"Are you sure?"

She blew smoke. "Of course I'm sure. My whole stupid Nancy Drew act was a failure. Every time I had a few minutes by myself I went through drawers, cabinets, closets, boxes, everything. I didn't find a damned thing."

"Then why did you call Norris Beamer?" Kendrake asked.

"For help. I thought maybe he knew something I could use, or at least that he had suspicions."

She'd been right about that, Finn thought. But his mind was still stuck on her previous statement.

"You can't really mean you didn't find anything suspicious," Finn said. "What about the arsenic under the kitchen sink?"

Through the haze of tobacco smoke Finn saw Sheila LaFeulle wrinkle her eyebrows. "I don't know what you're talking about. I looked under the sink every day I was there, when I emptied the trash can. I can assure you there wasn't any arsenic there the day before she died."

TWENTY-SEVEN

WHO IS LOIS KEELING?

"What do you make of that?" Kendrake asked Finn in the car.

"Nothing. It makes no sense. The arsenic had to be under the sink before the murder. The killer didn't put it there!"

"But why would Mrs. LaFeulle lie about that?"

Finn sighed. "I don't know. There's no reason, is there? Not even if she's the murderer."

"You don't think—"

"Not really. I think we're back to the lover."

As they drew near the A-Plus offices, Finn was surprised to see a man pacing outside. He was just under six feet tall, black, with a mustache and horn-rim glasses.

"Calvin!" Finn called out the window as they pulled up next to the man. "What brings you to the low-rent district?"

"Lunch," said Calvin Jefferson, chief investigator for the Cheviot Mutual Insurance Co., part-time preacher, and Finn's friend for nearly twenty years. "I was at Skyline Chili down the street and I thought I might as well come in and talk a little business."

Finn introduced him to Kendrake and they went inside.

"Cozy place you have here."

"Thanks," Finn said. "Watch out for the dog hair."

Calvin squinted at one of the chairs in front of Finn's desk, then sat. Kendrake took over the other chair and opened her spiral notebook.

"Remember calling me week before last with some suspicions about the death of one of our insureds, Otto Beamer?" Calvin asked.

What now? Finn thought. He licked his dry lips and looked at Kendrake in her white stockings and blue summer-weight suit. She raised a perfectly shaped eyebrow.

"I remember," Finn said.

"Now the wife's dead."

"We're well aware of that."

Calvin leaned forward. "It turns out that she has her own policy with Cheviot Mutual, for a hundred and fifty thousand dollars. Not huge, but a tidy sum for a woman in her income bracket."

"Who gets the money?" Kendrake asked, beating Finn to it.

"Thereby hangs a tale. The original beneficiary was her husband, and the policy was bought at the same time he named her in his policy. But she changed it after he died, as you would expect. The new beneficiary is a cousin named Lois Keeling. Sound familiar?"

Finn ran the name through the computer banks of his mind and came up a blank. He looked at Kendrake, who shrugged.

"I don't think so," Finn said. "Should it?"

"No, I was just hoping you'd know her. Nobody else does."

"What do you mean? Who is she?"

"That's what we don't know, Frank. We don't have an address on her and she doesn't show in the phone book. She may not be local at all. We don't know of any other relatives who can help us find her. Our people called Mrs. Beamer's stepson, but he was no help."

"Understandably." Beamer could scarcely be expected to know Viola's cousin. At the moment Finn regretted that, for he wanted very much for this Lois Keeling to be found. A beneficiary to the tune of a hundred and fifty thousand dollars would make an excellent murder suspect—much more believable than a vengeful stepson.

"Try Viola's lawyer," Finn suggested. "The one she gave that letter accusing Norris of her murder. Chances are good she named this same Lois Keeling in her will, and if she did, the lawyer ought to know where to find her."

"Mrs. Jefferson didn't raise any stupid kids. I thought of that. The lawyer is acting dumb, only I'm not sure it's acting. It's Corwin Liggett."

The man who was shaped like a light bulb but wasn't bright. "Oh, yeah, I forgot," Finn said. "Well, this is an intriguing problem. I enjoy missing persons cases."

"You mean you enjoy getting paid, but I think we can handle this one in-house."

Finn snorted. "If you really thought that, you wouldn't be here. Lunch was just an excuse. Calvin, I have a personal interest in finding this woman, so I'm going to make inquiries whether you pay me or not. But let me make you a proposition: If I find her before you do, I'll submit a bill which you don't have to pay unless you want to know what I know. What could be fairer? You can't lose."

He put out his hand. Calvin shook it.

"Good luck, Frank," he said. "I hope you do better on this than on that phony injury claim you've been nursing. When do I get to see that videotape you bragged about on the phone the other day?"

Finn cleared his throat. "There's a little problem with that, Calvin."

"What kind of problem?"

"Nothing I can't handle."

Finn wasn't finished yet with Hawley Smoot.

"Excuse me," Kendrake said after Calvin had gone, "but did I hear you just take on another case when we've already got two murders on tap? I know we need the money, but—"

"Not another case," Finn said. "The same one. When we find Lois Keeling, we find a person with a strong motive for killing Viola Beamer—stronger than Viola's unidentified boyfriend."

"Oh. Sure. It's a shame that Chandler already has an assignment. She'd be perfect for this."

"She'd be good," Finn corrected. "We'll be perfect."

"It would be a lot easier if we had a PC to search databases."

"We have the next best thing: My friend Len Peterka at Worldwide Investigations. He's the best skip tracer I ever saw, and he owes me a big favor. He'll use Worldwide's computer to get Lois Keeling's address, place of employment, and social security number from one of the credit reporting companies that sell information. Meanwhile, you look for a driver's license. I want every bit of information we can get."

"What if Keeling lives out of the state?"

"Then start calling other states."

Energized, Finn picked up the phone and began punching in the number for the local Worldwide franchise. Kendrake left his office, presumably to use the phone at her desk.

Len Peterka, a high school classmate of Finn's and an enthusiastic newlywed, was as accommodating as expected. Two years previously Finn had introduced him to the woman who was now Peterka's wife, an action which had been of nearly equal benefit to both men.

"Why don't you give up that ulcer farm and come work for me?" Len said, as an associate ran a database search. "I'll buy out your operation."

Finn couldn't stand Len's partner, Sam Danziger, who was always making cracks about Finn's shortness. Still, the offer to sell out was seductive. No more debts, no more headaches. It would be so easy to say yes. And so hard. Giving up A-Plus would mean that he had failed. Finn wasn't ready for that, not while he was still in the fight.

"I'll take a rain check on that, Len."

A few minutes later, Finn's notepad was loaded with a complete rundown on Lois Keeling. How galling that much of the information came from the same credit reporting agency that had branded Finn a bad credit risk.

He went to tell Kendrake what he had, but the reception room was empty. Puzzled yet unworried, he amused himself by pulling out the *Williams Directory*. He looked up the suburban Cincinnati address he had just been given for Lois Keeling. With the directory one could take an address, see who lived there, then look up that person's name to find out where he or she worked. In the case of Lois Keeling, Finn was just double-checking what he already knew from the computer... or thought he knew.

It didn't check out.

The directory identified the address as belonging to Addresses Unlimited, a nationwide chain offering mail drop and other business services. Why would Lois Keeling use an accommodation address for her personal credit cards? If that part of the information about her was phony, then—

Finn felt his heart racing as he picked up the White Pages and found the phone number for Cybernaut Electronics, Inc. Supposedly this was where Lois Keeling worked. He jabbed in the digits. A female voice answered with the name of the company on the ninth ring.

"Ms. Keeling, please," Finn said.

"I'm sorry; we don't have anybody here by that name."

"Has she left the company?"

"We never had anyone of that name working here."

"Are you sure?"

The irritation on the other end of the line was palpable. "This is a five-person company, and I'm the owner, and I don't even have anybody to answer the phone right now. Yes, I'm sure."

Finn, totally simpatico to her plight, thanked the harried businesswoman. He received a tart "you're welcome" and a click in his ear.

Fishy was too mild a word for this. False address, false employer—and that wasn't all. Finn was contemplating other irregularities in the paper (or rather, computer) trail on Lois Keeling when Kendrake came into his office an hour or more later.

"Where did you get to, Mrs. Kendrake?"

"Just now, Kinko's. Lois Keeling's driver's license is only two months old, but the bureaucrats at the Bureau of Motor Vehicles in Columbus wouldn't read it to me over the phone. I had to have them fax it to Kinko's. Three dollars, plus Kinko's charges." She consulted her notebook. "The information on the license shows that Keeling is fifty-five years old, brown hair, five-five, a hundred and ten pounds. Her social security number—"

Finn beat her to it, reading from his own notes.

"How did you know?"

"I've been busy myself," he explained. "And what you found and what I found both point in the same direction. How is it, for example, that a fifty-five-year-old woman is just now getting a driver's license?"

"Maybe she never had to drive before."

"That's not very likely in a city without decent mass transit. Especially when the same woman's entire credit history began only seven weeks ago. She has exactly one VISA purchase to her name. Her address is a mail drop and her supposed employers never heard of her. And here's something really cute." Finn pointed to the Society Security number on his yellow legal pad. "See those middle two digits, oh nine? Our friends at the Social Security Administration didn't start issuing cards with those numbers until just a few years ago. Her Social Security card is probably about as old as her driver's license and her VISA card. It's as if Lois Keeling didn't exist until May."

"Oh, she existed all right." Kendrake reached into her purse and brought out a folded sheet of paper. "I needed a date of birth to get the driver's license data, so I popped down to the Bureau of Vital Statistics and picked this up. That's why I was gone so long."

She handed Finn a photocopy of a birth certificate indicating that Lois Marie Keeling had been born at Good Samaritan Hospital in Cincinnati fifty-five years ago the previous February.

"It was the only Lois Keeling I could find in city or county records," Kendrake said. "There's no marriage license on file, for instance."

"How about a death certificate?"

Kendrake stared.

"One of the oldest ploys in the book. You look up the death certificates for X number of years ago until you find one who would have been the right age if she hadn't died as a child. Come back later and get a birth certificate for the poor child and you're all set. You can become that person, use the birth certificate for ID, and never worry about being challenged by the real person."

"Do you think—"

"I'll find out." Finn grabbed the phone. "Did you see a good-looking blonde at Vital Statistics, about forty, well-build, perky?" He punched in a phone number from memory while he talked.

"Sounds familiar."

"She'll tell me anything."

On the other end of the phone, Finn heard a nasal, "Vital Statistics."

"Is Becky Shanks in, please?"

She was. Finn waited for her to come to the phone, wondering how to explain not having called her in more weeks than he could count on both hands.

"Hello?"

"Becky, honey, this is Finn."

"Finn who?"

Uh-oh. "Finn who wants to take you to dinner at the Maisonette, that's Finn who." It was the only five-star restaurant in Cincinnati.

Kendrake raised an eyebrow.

"You scoundrel," Becky said, a word that mirrored the look on Kendrake's face. "If you think you can just march back into my life like you owned it and bribe me with an expensive dinner at... What night?"

They negotiated and settled on Tuesday. Maybe Finn's efforts to elude Becky's romantic designs would take his mind off the catastrophic deadline that arrived that day. Finn liked women. He liked them very much. But he liked his independence even more.

"Don't hang up," he said after the date was settled. "I need a minuscule favor first."

"I thought it would come down to that! Francis, you never change."

"Part of my charm."

"What is it this time?"

Finn asked her to check if there was a death certificate for a Lois Marie Keeling, probably an infant or child. She promised to call back in a few moments.

"That was outrageous exploitation of that woman," Kendrake said when he hung up. "You should be ashamed of yourself."

Finn snorted. "Save your sympathy for somebody who needs it. Becky Shanks is as defenseless as a boa constrictor and about as hard to get away from." His face brightened. "Maybe you'd like to join us for dinner. You'd like Becky."

She shook her head. "No, thanks. You do realize that you could have just sent me back to Vital Statistics and saved the price of a five-star dinner? Or were you just giving yourself an excuse for calling her?"

Actually, he'd been showing off. But before Finn could find a way to defend himself without admitting that, the phone rang.

"Bingo," Becky told him. "Lois Marie Keeling died of spinal meningitis at the age of five months. Poor kid." She read him the death date.

"Great work," Finn said. "I really appreciate this."

"I'll tell you a secret, Francis. I would have done you the favor for old times' sake, without a bribe. But you're stuck now. See you Tuesday."

Despite the mild dig, Finn smiled as he hung up.

"I knew it," he told Kendrake. "Viola Beamer's beneficiary is a fabrication, a figment of somebody's imagination—and I know whose. Look at that description of Lois Keeling on her driver's license. The age, the hair. Who does that sound like?"

Kendrake shrugged. "The only one I can think of is Viola Beamer herself."

"Exactly." Finn stood, too agitated to sit any longer. "Viola Beamer created a false identity that she named in her insurance policy as her own beneficiary."

"But why?"

"So she could pretend to die and still make money on the deal. The matrimony-cum-homicide scheme couldn't continue indefinitely without somebody getting wise, so she probably planned this method of retirement before she killed Otto Beamer. 'Dying' was a perfect way to get anyone off her track—or so she thought. The insurance settlement would give her new identity an excuse for having substantial funds. In reality she would have far more than that, with her blood money transferred to accounts in the Lois Keeling name."

"But Smoot saw Viola's body," Kendrake objected.

"Smooth saw *a* body. For all we know it could have been"—he searched for an example—"the woman missing from the nursing home." Finn stopped, struck by his own words. "Yes, *the woman from the nursing home*! Suppose Viola and her accomplice kidnapped Virginia Hartwell, dyed her hair brown like Viola's, and shot her. That would silence her *and* provide the necessary body. I don't know who ID'd the deceased, but it had to be somebody who didn't know Viola all that well. A misidentification could be counted on. The police wouldn't check the fingerprints because there was no real doubt about the identity of the victim."

"And I bet the body will be cremated."

"Not if we hurry," Finn said. "Call the coroner's office and find out if it's been released to a funeral home yet. If the body isn't Viola, then the whole case against Norris Beamer collapses."

TWENTY-EIGHT

INTIMATE IMAGES

Rosalee Chandler shifted uneasily as she rode the elevator of the downtown building where Intimate Images was located. Paper documents and computer files and even indifferent government clerks she could handle. But never before had she taken on an assignment like this for the A-Plus Detective Agency. She was to interview someone person-to-person, not taxpayer-to-bureaucrat. And not only that, Hilary Kendrake said Mr. Finn thought somebody in this business might be involved in Viola Beamer's murder. The victim had phoned Intimate Images several times in the last two weeks before she died.

At first Chandler refused the job. But in the end she just couldn't say no to Mrs. Kendrake. That would be letting her down, and she couldn't let down a woman she had grown to admire in the very short time she had known her. Chandler would get through this by trying to be like her. She was sure that Mrs. Kendrake didn't know what it was like to be awkward or afraid. Or for men to think that she was dull. How she would love to have Mrs. Kendrake's poise and self-confidence!

With a lurch that unsettled her already-queasy innards, the ancient elevator deposited Chandler on the ninth floor. She walked down a long, musty hallway, turned right and then right again before encountering a frosted glass door with "DOUG WINFIELD PHOTOGRAPHY" painted on it and "INTIMATE IMAGES" below that. Chandler ran a hand through her hair, smoothed her skirt, and told the butterflies in her stomach to fly away. She opened the door and walked in.

The small reception desk was abandoned. It looked like her dentist's waiting room, except that the magazines sitting on the glass end tables weren't four years old. Another difference was the photographs on the walls—a gallery of dreamy-eyed women in peek-a-boo lingerie, displaying bare shoulders or bare backs in provocative poses. They were like pictures out of those Victoria's Secret catalogs that Mr. Finn peeked at when he thought no one was looking!

Chandler sat down and flipped through *Cosmopolitan*, hoping the Doug Winfield whose name was on the door would show up before her lunch hour was over. Otherwise, she'd have to go through this all over again.

But what if he appeared and didn't want to talk to her about Viola Beamer? The subtle approach, Chandler decided; that's what Mr. Finn would counsel.

"Hi, there."

Chandler's hands twitched at the sudden sound and she dropped the magazine.

"How are you today?" The speaker, walking into the waiting area from some back room, was a man about her own age with bright red hair gathered into a pony tail, tied with a black ribbon. He wore a white silk shirt, open at the collar, and black pants.

"I'm wonderful." Chandler bent down and picked up the magazine without taking her eyes off the man. *He looks like Thomas Jefferson, only much sexier*, she thought wildly.

"I'm Doug Winfield. You don't have an appointment, do you?"

"Rosalee Chandler." She hopped to her feet. "I sort of came on impulse."

"Well, you're lucky." He clapped his hands together. "I happen to have a few minutes free if you'd like to talk about setting up a photo session. How did you find out about me?"

"From a... friend. Viola Beamer."

Winfield's cheerful expression turned serious. "I heard about her murder on the news. What a tragedy. Let's go in back and talk about what you have in mind."

As she followed him down a hallway, past a closed door, Chandler asked: "Did you know Viola very well?"

"Only met her a few times. Called her last week to let her know her photos were ready, but she never picked them up. She was killed the next day."

Winfield led Chandler into a small room, no windows, with two or three floor lights and phony backdrops that pulled down like window shades. He invited her to sit on a long couch while he settled himself on a stool in front of a cozy fireplace scene.

"Most women are a little hesitant about this and I try to set their minds at rest," he said, "but you seem even more nervous than most."

"Nervous?" Chandler croaked. "Why should I be nervous?"

"No reason at all. That's the spirit! When we get into the photo session, I want you to think of me as being like a doctor, except that I won't ask you to take all your clothes off—only as many as you want."

"I don't intend to take *any* of my clothes off!"

She hated that she squirmed, but she couldn't help it.

"Boy, you *are* nervous. But that's okay. You can wear a sweatshirt and jeans if you want. Whatever turns your man on. You can even bring him to the photo session if that makes you feel more comfortable."

"I don't have a man."

Winfield held up his hands. "Hey, your sexual preference, if any, is none of my business."

Chandler colored. "I mean I don't have a boyfriend at the moment." Now she understood the persistence of the lingerie motif in those waiting-room photos. "This is one of those sleazy boudoir photography places, isn't it?"

Winfield leapt from the stool. "There's nothing sleazy about it. Intimate Images tries to bring out the beauty, the vitality, the sensuality in every woman for that special man in her life in the way that most appeals to him. Maximum skin is not the name of the game in this shop. Most of what I do, you could show your mother without embarrassment."

Chandler leaned backward on the sofa as Winfield got closer. "That's good to hear, but I just wanted a—a passport photo."

He chuckled. "I can do that, of course, but I assumed you wanted something like what your friend got."

"Viola? She had a boudoir photo taken? I'd sure like to see it."

"That would hardly be professional of me, showing clients' pictures without their permission, would it?"

"No, I suppose not, as a general thing. But we *were* friends and she *is* dead." Chandler put on what she hoped was her most persuasive smile.

"I don't know…"

"Maybe I'd like it so much I'd want one."

"Wait a minute."

So much for professional ethics, Chandler thought.

Winfield ducked into an adjacent room and brought out an eight-by-ten color portrait. The subject sat in a tiger-like crouch, hands on the floor, leaning forward so that her breasts almost hung out of the front of her peach teddy. From her neck dangled a pedant in a shape Chandler recognized as the ancient Egyptian symbol for life. Viola's body was firm and shapely; she didn't look like a woman in her fifties. The expression on her face was one that Chandler saw in a million magazine ads—that far-away, wet-lips look.

"Wow," she said. "Set this picture on some guy's desk and I bet it would really brighten his day. I didn't even know Viola had a boyfriend. Did he come in with her?"

Winfield shook his head. "Never saw him."

"Did she mention his name? Maybe he's somebody I know."

A name would accomplish Chandler's mission in high style, but Winfield couldn't provide one. According to him, Viola had only talked coyly about raising the temperature of "my playmate." Chandler tried not to look sick.

"So should I schedule you for a shoot?"

"You do very good work, Mr. Winfield, but I don't think I have any use for a photo like that."

"It doesn't have to be a desk photo, you know. Once you've paid the fee for the session, we could turn your picture into a calendar for an extra two hundred and seventy-five dollars."

Chandler stood up. "Thanks, but no thanks."

"The Intimate Images jigsaw puzzle is only thirty-five dollars. I'll throw it in for free if you have dinner with me tonight."

He couldn't mean it. Chandler cleared her throat. "Is that a special?"

"Very special."

He must be trying to take her mind off Viola Beamer, Chandler decided. What would Mr. Finn do in this situation? Or Mrs. Kendrake? "Do you have any literature about all of these options?"

"All but the dinner. Be right back."

What should she do now? Whatever she wasn't supposed to do, she reasoned. As Winfield disappeared down the hallway, she headed in the other direction and across the hall. The closed door she passed earlier said "DARKROOM" and below that "KEEP CLOSED." Chandler opened the door and went in. She couldn't believe she was doing this.

An unpleasant smell assaulted her nose. The stuff used in developing photographs, no doubt. Chandler knew nothing about photography. Bathed in the glow of an amber light she could see what she presumed were developing tanks, jars of white chemicals, photography equipment...

Chemicals.

Poisons were chemicals, and Mrs. Kendrake had told Chandler that Otto Beamer had been poisoned.

She took a step farther into the darkroom.

But a firm grip on her upper arm stopped her.

* * * * *

Canova parked his Mustang in front of the house across the street from the Beamers' place. This was where their best witness lived.

As he and Barkeloo got out of his car, he saw the garage door of the Beamers' house go up. A man came out. Blond-haired, just under six feet tall, wearing a short-sleeve white shirt and tie. He had something under his arm—a sign, it looked like.

Canova crossed the street. He approached the man as he was closing the garage door.

"Afternoon."

The man whirled around. "Oh. Hi. You startled me."

Greylock had been way off on the age. This dude looked more like forty than late twenties. "You must be Mrs. Beamer's son."

"What gives you that idea?"

"You're coming out of her house."

"I'm her real estate agent. She contracted to sell the home, but of course that's on hold now. This was the first day the police tape was down, and I could get my sign back. Are you from the police?"

Canova looked at the FOR SALE sign in the other man's hand. It said *Landmark Realtors* on top and *Bill Longdale* down below, with two telephone numbers.

"My name is Canova. I'm an investigator with Cheviot Mutual Insurance." That was almost sort of true. "This is Ms. Barkeloo. We're trying to find out a little about Mrs. Beamer's son. Do you know him?"

Longdale shook his head. "Didn't know she had one." *She didn't, pal.* "I wish you wouldn't stir things up. A murder in this neighborhood is terrible for property values. It doesn't project a very positive image."

"I guess that makes two reasons for Mrs. Beamer to be sorry it happened. Look, we just want to ask a few questions. We'll knock on doors until I find somebody who met this son."

"Don't do that! You might induce panic selling." Longdale started walking down the driveway with his sign, away from Canova and Barkeloo. "You can talk to my mom. She probably knows something. Bessie Longdale. She lives right there." He nodded in the direction of the house across the street. "Just watch out for her dog."

TWENTY-NINE

ASHES TO ASHES

"Viola must be a creature of habit," Kendrake said as they pulled up in front of the Eternal Rest Funeral Home. "She's having 'herself' buried from the same place that did the honors for Otto Beamer."

"Maybe she got a volume discount," Finn muttered as he unbuckled his seat belt.

The call to the coroner's office established that the body identified as Viola Beamer already had been autopsied and released to Eternal Rest.

Apparently, an afternoon visitation was in progress at the funeral home, for several other couples and individuals walked up the front path at the same time as Finn and Kendrake. Finn smiled his gratitude at a prune-faced man with a hearing aid who held the door open for him.

Finn had never been in the Colonial-style building, but he felt as though he had. From reading the purple prose of Joe Canova's report, painstaking in its irrelevant and ungrammatical detail, he knew that he would find the funeral director's offices to the left of the entrance hallway.

The outer office, with its businesslike metal desk and matching file cabinets, was unattended. Finn and Kendrake went through the adjoining door, which stood ajar.

Behind a mahogany desk that dominated the room, a pale man in a dark beard—presumably funeral director Samuel Greylock—was talking on the phone. When he saw Finn and Kendrake, he scowled but kept talking:

"But our aggressive advertising campaign has had impressive results already."

Finn looked around. It was, as Canova had indicated, a class room: hardwood floor, Oriental rug, antiques, Jesus in stained glass, paintings on the wall.

"The profit margin at this unit was up substantially in the second quarter, as you'll see when you get the figures."

To the right and behind the man on the phone was the mummified dog which Canova had described in his report. In front of it stood something even stranger, which he hadn't—a human-sized sarcophagus. At least, that's how it was shaped. But this was nothing like King Tut's: It was fashioned out of shiny metal. Kendrake approached to study it up close.

Greylock put his hand over the mouthpiece of the phone and spoke pointedly. "The Klemperer visitation is across the hall."

"Thanks," Finn said, "but we're here to see you."

Greylock took his hand off the mouthpiece and spoke into the phone again. "I have unannounced visitors, Phil. May I call you back? Thanks."

He cradled the phone with a thump of plastic upon plastic. His eyes were ice blue. "How may I help you?"

"We understand from the coroner's office that you're handling the arrangements for the body of the late Viola Beamer," Finn said.

"That's correct, but I'm afraid there will be no visitation and no service."

"Nevertheless, we'd like to see the body."

"I'm sorry, but that's not possible." Greylock didn't look sorry, Finn noticed. "And who do you think you are, barging into my office and—"

Before he had even begun the challenge, Finn was reaching into his breast pocket for the disingenuous answer. He pulled out a leather case and flashed the gold badge inside. It looked official, although it said "PRIVATE" at the top of the eagle and "DETEC-TVE" below. Finn held it from the top, covering the adjective with his fingers.

"Detective Finn," he said. He nodded toward Kendrake. "This woman is on temporary assignment to my office." He had already warned her not to roll her eyes at this true but misleading introduction.

"I don't care who you are," Greylock snapped. "You still can't see Mrs. Beamer. She's already been sent on to Birnbaum Chapel."

The news hit Finn with the force of an ocean wave. "Isn't that the crematorium?"

"That's right." Greylock wrinkled his nose in disgust. "Mrs. Beamer left instructions with her attorney that she wished to be cremated, like her late husband."

"Husbands," Kendrake corrected from where she was standing by the metal sarcophagus. "She had at least five who were cremated, conveniently removing any evidence of foul play."

Greylock eyed her appraisingly, then shook his head. "A private investigator told me there was some suspicion of murder. I tried to help him, but—"

"It's gone beyond suspicion," Finn said. "I haven't the slightest doubt that Viola Beamer is a multiple murderer."

"If that's true, it's ironic that someone murdered her as well."

"It would be, all right, but we don't think she was murdered. We don't even think she's dead."

Greylock gaped at Finn, then shook his head. "Of course she's dead. I saw her body myself before we sent it to the crematorium."

"Are you sure that was the same woman who came here to make the arrangements for her husband's funeral?" Finn asked.

"I never questioned it."

"Question it now."

Greylock appeared to think. "She looked like Mrs. Beamer to me."

"How can you be sure," Kendrake asked, "considering that the woman was shot in the head?"

"I didn't say I was sure. I said she looked like Mrs. Beamer to me. That's the best I can do. Now, what else can I tell you?"

Kendrake pointed to the sarcophagus. "Is this what it appears to be?"

Greylock nodded. "Yes, indeed. Stainless steel. Not very decorative, but intensely practical."

"I mean, is there a mummy in there?"

"Oh, no, not yet." In a surprising burst of animation, Greylock left his desk and opened the metal case by way of demonstration. It didn't look to Finn like a roomy place to spend eternity, but then a coffin wasn't exactly a three-room suite, either.

"I could put you in this for twelve thousand dollars," Greylock told Kendrake. "Of course, that's in addition to a mummification fee of—"

"Wait a minute," Finn interrupted, determined to get back on track. "When do you think the crematorium will, uh, deal with Viola's body?"

Greylock shrugged his shoulders, denting the smooth outlines of his blue suit. "I don't know exactly. But it certainly will be taken care of sometime today, if it hasn't been done already."

Finn and Kendrake were out of his office before he finished the last sentence.

* * * * *

"Not ashes," said William Dennert, the general manager of Birnbaum Chapel. A stout man with closely cropped gray hair, he gripped his red suspenders and shook his head. "That's a common misconception. Mrs. Beamer won't be reduced to ashes, as you put it. Nobody ever is. This is a modern, clean-burning process. What you get after burning a body at eighteen hundred degrees is a bunch of bone fragments five, maybe six inches long. Then we break them down into smaller pieces. That's the cremains. People just think they're ashes."

"*Cremains?*" Finn wiped his forehead. "You're missing the point here, Mr. Dennert. We don't care what's left when you're finished. What we really want to know is, has Mrs. Beamer been cremated yet?"

Dennert shrugged. "I don't know. That's usually done right after the memorial service, but in her case there wasn't one. Let's go see."

He led Finn and Kendrake to an elevator and pushed the "down" button. Apparently impressed by Finn's gold badge, Dennert showed every indication of being helpful. What he did not show was any hurry about it. He moved at the pace of a man who is reminded by his daily work that time is an illusion and eternity is for real. He also talked non-stop about his job.

"Some relatives like to watch," he said in the elevator. "Especially families from India. In this country it's the closest they can get to a funeral pyre, you know. One time a couple of years back…"

It was the longest elevator trip Finn ever experienced.

When the elevator doors opened again, the first thing Finn saw was a man in a flowered shirt standing in front of one of three chambers built into the wall at the far end of the basement.

The combustion chambers.

Just as Finn's brain registered his presence, the man bent down in front of two small windows in a metal door and pushed a button.

The truth about who resided in Viola Beamer's casket was about to go up in smoke! Finn grabbed Dennert and shouted in his face. "Stop it, man! Make him turn that thing off!"

"Don't get excited." Dennert cupped his hands around his mouth. "Hey, Randy! That Mrs. Beamer in there?"

Randy took a cigar out of his mouth. "Naw. She's next." He pointed with the cigar to a coffin next to him, resting on a gurney with wheels.

Kendrake's long legs enabled her to beat Finn to the gurney, but only by seconds.

As they flipped up the brass latches on the side of the metal casket, Finn wondered why coffins had them. The latches kept nobody out, and there was no need to keep anybody in.

"We never disturb the casket in the cremation process," Dennert protested as he ambled up beside his two visitors.

"Admirable." Finn looked at Kendrake, who was holding the other side of the casket lid. He thought he detected a slight pallor in her cheeks. "Is this going to bother you?"

"I'm okay."

Of course she's okay. Finn mentally kicked himself. The woman once had to identify her own husband lying stone cold dead at the hands of a madman.

They lifted the lid.

The woman who lay in the casket as though asleep wore a nightgown and a necklace. Her dyed brown hair was brushed over the right side of the face in such a way that it covered the bullet holes above her eye and ear. The Eternal Rest Funeral Home had done a nice job on the face, even though there was no visitation. Why? Who paid for that?

Nevertheless, she looked dead. Finn had never seen a corpse that didn't, no matter how deftly prepared by the undertaker. There was an unnaturalness to a dead body that wasn't eliminated by a mortician's work. For that reason, plus the fact that he had never seen the murderess in the flesh, Finn was confronted by an unexpected complication: He couldn't say whether this was Viola Beamer or not.

"What do you think?" he asked Kendrake.

She bit her lip in concentration. "I'm not sure. From the picture I saw in the newspaper, it looks like Mrs. Beamer. But I couldn't swear to it. We'll have to get the police to use fingerprints and dental records."

"Sure it's Mrs. Beamer," Dennert said.

Finn, having forgotten the professional's presence, jerked around. "How can you be so certain?"

"Because I knew her. Real well. Every time one of her husbands died, she'd bring him here. She was one of the ones who always watched. I used to joke that she was my steadiest customer. She didn't like jokes much, though."

"Too bad." Finn emitted a heavy sigh as he and Kendrake lowered the lid onto the coffin. "This joke's on us."

* * * * *

The Rottweiler ran from the back yard and barked furiously when Canova and Barkeloo came out of Bessie Longdale's house. Canova was sure he was barking at him, and he had no confidence in the old adage about barks versus bites.

"Look out," Canova yelled, even though Barkeloo was only a foot away from him. "That's not a dog, it's a freaking Hound of the Baskervilles!"

Barkeloo appeared to ignore him as she knelt down in the grass. "Come here, doggie. Good doggie!" The dog paddled up to her. She giggled as he licked her face.

"I'm sorry to ruin your play time," Canova said acidly, "but I've got to get going."

"What's the hurry?"

"Something's screwy, doesn't match."

"The different descriptions of the boyfriend, you mean?"

"You noticed that?" Canova asked, impressed.

"Of course. I'm not stupid." *You learn something new every day*, he thought. "So where are you going, Joe?"

He told her.

"I'll go with you."

"No." He tried to sound brave. "It might be dangerous. You could break a fingernail or something."

"Ha-ha." But she looked at her nails, carefully painted the same shade of yellow as her halter top.

Canova didn't want to burn any bridges with her, but he also wanted to close the case by himself.

"Tell you what: Wait for me at the Blue Lagoon. If I don't show up in an hour, come rescue me."

He thought he was kidding.

THIRTY

REFLECTIONS IN A PITCHER OF BEER

"If I had any hair left," Finn said, "I'd pull it out."

He sat at his desk, head in hand, looking lost and weary. Kendrake missed the old Finn, the dreamer and schemer, romantic and rogue. His enthusiasm made the job worthwhile, made her want to help this crazy school for sleuths survive. She still wanted to. Her interest now went beyond the feeling that it was nice to be needed. Kendrake cared what happened to Francis Aloysius Finn, she admitted to herself.

"Maybe it didn't work out," she said, "but it was still a good theory."

"Good?" Finn snorted. "It was bloody brilliant. It was perfect!" He slapped the table. "But it was wrong. And if we can't solve a case with almost the entire Famous Detectives School mobilized on it, then we're sunk as an agency, even if we weren't about to lose our license."

He pulled out a cigar and lit it, a sign of life that Kendrake found encouraging (albeit noxious). She filed some folders and tried not to choke while Finn smoked in silence.

"Viola's lover-cum-accomplice is still the key," he announced finally. "Why haven't we heard from Chandler? Or Canova? They should have called in by now."

"Maybe they haven't had a chance to conduct their interviews yet. I don't think it's anything to worry about."

"No, of course not. Who's worried?"

But Kendrake detected a level of anxiety unusual in her boss. With nothing left to do at the moment, Finn was unraveling at the edges.

"Maybe we've missed something," she suggested. "If Viola's sweetheart isn't at that Intimate Images business Chandler's checking, he could be one of the other names on that list of cellular phone calls."

She found the yellow sheet on Finn's desk and shoved it in front of him. "Corwin Liggett, for instance. There could have been more than just an attorney-client relationship there."

"Based on what— Viola's sympathy for animal rights? I think we can rule out sexual attraction. Plus, he barely scratches out a living in the least prestigious areas of the law and doesn't have the brains to pass a urine test."

"Sounds to me as if he's just the sort of man a woman like her could get to do her dirty work by pretending to be in love."

Finn puffed on his cigar meditatively. "You know, that actually makes a lot of psychological sense. But you've forgotten that lover boy passed himself off as Viola's son. Corwin's by far the wrong age and body shape."

He glanced down at the paper. "If only that Mrs. Longdale person—"

Kendrake leaped at the sound of the front door bell. In the reception area she found two visitors: Rosalee Chandler and a young man with red hair. When Kendrake returned to Finn's office with the couple in tow, the detective lit up as if the burden of Atlas had been lifted from his shoulders.

"Ms. Chandler! I knew I could count on you. What did you find out?"

She nodded in the direction of her companion. "Let me introduce Doug Winfield. He's a photographer and he owns Intimate Images. He caught me sneaking into his darkroom, so I had to tell him everything. Viola Beamer was a customer of his—"

"One of hundreds. I didn't really know her."

Finn just looked at Winfield and stuck his cigar into his mouth. The Silent Treatment, Kendrake realized. That had been covered in Lesson Two, "How to Get Anybody to Talk About Anything." But Winfield didn't crack under Finn's steady gaze. It was Chandler who broke the silence.

"Doug took a sexy picture of Mrs. Beamer to give her boyfriend, that's all," she said. "He's an excellent photographer. Here, see for yourself."

She handed Finn an eight-by-ten. Kendrake, standing next to Finn's desk, twisted her head for a look at the photo. It was eerie to see Viola Beamer dressed in slinky nightwear, an erotic expression on her face and an inviting pose to her body. Less than two hours before, Kendrake and Finn had seen that same body lying cold and lifeless in a casket. And by now it must be reduced to five or six pounds of ashes—*no*, bone fragments—contained in an urn about the size of a sack of flour.

"Why were you talking to her on the phone the day before she died?" Finn asked in a neutral voice.

"How do you know I was?"

"Why are you evading the question?"

"I'm not. I'm just curious. Anyway, her photos were ready. That's the answer to your question."

"That wouldn't take that long to tell her. Why did she have to call you back?"

"I was in the middle of explaining a special sale price to her when she was interrupted. When she called back she wound up buying the jigsaw puzzle version for her boyfriend as well as the eight-by-ten. I still have her bill."

He pulled it out of his shirt pocket and held it up.

"Did you get this boyfriend's name?" Finn asked in a strangled voice.

Winfield shook his head.

Finn heaved a sigh from the depths of his soul and looked at Kendrake. "I need a drink. I need a lot of drinks."

* * * * *

At Finn's insistence, Kendrake shut the office and went with him to a nearby bar. It was late afternoon. The place was called The Office, Finn explained, so that patrons could phone their spouses and say they were staying late at The Office without lying.

"You do realize that nobody really falls for that, don't you, Mr. Finn?"

"They pretend to. That's good enough."

The old wood-frame building had cheap paneling, a compact disc juke box, and the longest bar in Greater Cincinnati. Finn contended that it also had the coldest beer. He ordered a pitcher of Hudepohl beer and bought Kendrake a Diet Coke.

A dark-haired woman in her late twenties, showing an immense expanse of thigh under pink short-shorts, brought them their drinks and took away an ashtray full of peanut shells left by an earlier patron.

"Smart woman, Molly." Finn followed her legs as she sauntered away. "She's the owner."

"I'm sure she aced business school." Kendrake leaned forward, determined to redirect Finn's thoughts into more constructive channels. "What do you normally do when you hit a brick wall on a case? Other than consume beer, I mean?"

"Start over." The little detective put a pen to napkin. "I'm going to write down every candidate for Viola's unknown lover."

In half a minute he had written:

Gus Hackleshin
Bessie Longdale's son
Doug Winfield
Richard Chavez

"But we've already ruled out Winfield and Chavez," Kendrake said, "and you've never taken the others seriously."

"I also said we're starting over. Maybe we were too hasty. We don't have any real evidence it's not one of them."

"You told me Chavez is close to Viola's age. He couldn't have been the man posing as her son any more than William Longdale could have. And why would he tell you about the digitalis if he was her accomplice in her husband's murder?"

"She could have had more than one lover—her partner and somebody else. I just thought of that. And her own murder could have been the result of jealousy, a love triangle. That's why I included Longdale and Hackleshin."

"Then shouldn't you include Corwin Liggett?"

After a long pause, Finn threw down his pen. "This is futile. If she had twelve boyfriends, we might not have come across any of them in our investigation. We have to go about this in a different way."

"Such as?"

"Rethink everything. Challenge assumptions. Look for things that don't make sense."

Kendrake thought a moment. "I'll tell you what doesn't make sense, Mr. Finn. Why did Viola stay in this town? She was running an awful risk of somebody noticing the mortality rate of her husbands. What kept her here?"

Finn shrugged. "The boyfriend, maybe."

"Then what kept *him* here?"

"That's a good question." Finn took a healthy swig of his amber beverage while he thought. "There must be something he can do better here than in another city, probably something that was a help to Viola's homicidal habits." He set down his glass as he spoke with increasing excitement. "Maybe our reports from the field—"

"I have them right here." Kendrake picked up the attaché-size purse she had set by the metal legs of her chair. "I was hoping you'd get bored with drinking." She pulled out a thick wad of folders and papers, topped by the studio photo of Viola Beamer.

"Mrs. Kendrake, you are a remarkable woman."

That would have meant more to her if Finn hadn't said it with the sloppy sentimentality of the two-drink drunk that he was fast becoming.

He took the pile of material. But instead of diving into the folders as Kendrake expected, he seemed mesmerized by the photograph—almost as if it were a Victoria's Secret catalog.

He pointed at the gold pendant nestled between Viola's ample breasts. "Wasn't that on the body at the crematorium?"

"Oh, yes. Why?"

"Because it must have been important to her boyfriend, since it's almost the only thing she's wearing. Maybe he gave it to her. We could send one of our student sleuths to all the jewelry shops that sell— Wait a minute. That design on the pendant. What's it called?"

"That's an ankh. It's an Egyptian symbol for life, ironically enough."

Finn seemed to have no time for irony. Without comment, he flipped through the stack of files until he found the folder containing reports from Chandler.

"What are you looking for?"

"The death notices." Finn pulled out the stack of white-on-black microfilm copies of death notices for Viola's late husbands. Kendrake peered over his shoulder just as he got to the second one:

HUNNICUT

William G., beloved husband of Viola Hunnicut (née Squires), loving father of Stephen Hunnicut of Atlanta and Sally Hunnicut Kinsey of Rochester, N.Y., loving grandfather of Michael, Jennifer and Gary Hunnicut and of Paul and Margaret Kinsey, past Grand Knight of Elder Council, past Faithful Navigator of the St. Isaac Jogues 4th Degree Knights of Columbus. Friday, November 15. Age 76. Mass of Christian Burial will be Tuesday, November 18 at 1 P.M. at St. Margaret of Cartona Church, Hyde Park. Visitation from 5 to 8 P.M. at the Eternal Rest Funeral Home, 1135 Schaefer Pike. Memorial contribution to the charity of one's choice would be appreciated.

Finn glanced through the other obits, spending no more than a few seconds on each. When he'd finished, he smacked the table, drawing looks from the other three world-weary bar patrons.

"Just as I thought."

"What, Mr. Finn?"

"Your question was brilliant, that's what. You solved the case, Mrs. Kendrake! The description would seal it." Finn was talking more to himself than to Kendrake now. "Why doesn't Joe Canova call with the description? Maybe Funderburgh knows. We never asked him. Big mistake, that."

"Never asked him what?" Kendrake's voice rose. Finn was making no sense. Maybe the beer affected him even more than she thought.

Finn stared at her, as if she were the one making no sense. "What Viola's 'son' looked like," he said, as though that were obvious. "It's not in the report, so we assumed Funderburgh didn't know. But maybe the neighbor told him, and he just didn't think it was important enough to pass on. I'll call him at the rest home where he's cavorting with Mrs. Pertwee."

"At their age, I'm not sure it's called cavorting."

The detective stood, unsteadily, and made his way to a pay phone near the rest rooms. In less than a minute he was back, smiling and flushed with triumph, as well as alcohol.

"Just as I suspected." He slurred the s's slightly. "Viola Beamer's phony son looked like one of the Smith Brothers on the cough drop box, according to Bessie Longdale. In other words, he had a beard."

THIRTY-ONE

THE STAINLESS STEEL SARCOPHAGUS

Kendrake insisted on driving, so they took her Volvo to the Eternal Rest Funeral Home.

She parked behind a red Mustang. Something seemed familiar about that car, Finn thought as they charged up the front walk of the funeral home, but he couldn't place it. *Maybe I shouldn't have had that last drink*, he thought. *Maybe I shouldn't have had the first one, either.*

The duo barged into the funeral director's office.

The reception area was deserted, and the inner door closed. Finn pounded on the door.

"Just a minute."

But it was much more than a minute before Samuel Greylock flung open the door. When he did, all Finn could focus on was his beard—closely cropped, brown, spade-shaped as it wrapped around his angular face. Not the way he remembered the Smith Brothers, but it was a long time since his mother bought him wild cherry cough drops.

"You again!" Greylock exclaimed. His suit was slightly askew, and he was breathing harder than one would expect from a man coming out of his office. "I'm too busy to talk right now. You'll have to excuse me."

Without waiting for a response, he retreated behind his desk and began shuffling paperwork from a standing position.

Finn and Kendrake followed him into the room.

"We made it to the crematorium in time to see the body," Finn said. "It was Viola Beamer, as advertised."

Greylock straightened his tie. "Then your clever theory about a substitution of bodies was wrong. How unfortunate."

Finn shook his head. "No, the theory was right. It's just that the plan didn't get carried out the way Viola expected. She intended to fake her death, all right, hanging the blame on Norris Beamer. There was an element of genius in that, because it did so much for the schemers: Using the nosy Virginia Hartwell as the substitute corpse would cover their tracks on the stolen digitalis. Then Viola's supposed death would make everyone lose interest in her homicidal history. Norris Beamer certainly would be in no position to make anybody interested—he'd be fighting a murder charge. And Viola's black widow routine supplied the motive for Norris, so no defense attorney in his right mind would want the cops looking too closely at that.

"Viola, meanwhile, would surface under a carefully prepared new identity to collect a hefty insurance settlement as the beneficiary of her own death."

Kendrake squeezed Finn's arm as if to warn him he was talking too fast and too much, but he couldn't stop himself. This was his grand moment of triumph. Finn had solved the murder of Viola Beamer. He had saved his client from prison or death. He had guaranteed that Beamer would be able to pay Finn's fees. He was a little tipsy.

"That was the plan," Finn pushed on. "But you had a better idea, Greylock, once you knew that someone was on to Viola. You realized you'd be safer if she was really dead and unable to testify against you."

"Me?" Greylock looked from Finn to Kendrake with a fair imitation of shock on his face. "Is this man drunk?"

Not at all sure how she would answer that, Finn cut in: "You were her business partner all these years, Greylock. Probably her lover, too, but at least her partner."

"I only met the woman when her husband died."

"That's what you told Joe Canova. But you also told him you'd been the director here for twelve years. Viola Beamer buried five of her six husbands during that period—and all five death notices show Eternal Rest as the funeral home. Sometimes an alert mortician spots something a coroner misses, but she didn't have to worry about that with the funeral director in on the scheme. That's why she stayed in the Cincinnati area, despite the risk that somebody here might notice the high mortality rate of her husbands."

Greylock shook his head. "We service hundreds of bereaved families every year. I can't remember them all." He narrowed his eyes. "And how do the police know what I told that private investigator?"

"We aren't the police," Finn said. "Sorry if you somehow got that impression. We're the A-Plus Detective Agency."

From the look Kendrake gave him, Finn dimly perceived that this was an unfortunate correction. Nevertheless, he forged on:

"Mr. Canova, perhaps unwisely, told you we were investigating Mrs. Beamer; you said so yourself the last time we were here. I suspect he also told you that her stepson was our client—which is why you framed Norris for Viola's murder, hoping to eliminate the threat from him permanently."

Greylock sat down behind his desk, a vacant look on his face. "Is that your idea of evidence?"

"Part of it. We also have a boudoir photo of Viola Beamer that she had taken just for you. She's wearing an Egyptian pendant around her neck." Finn waved vaguely at the painting of the pyramid-shaped mausoleum on the wall and at the stainless steel sarcophagus to the right of the desk. "With your fixation on the Egyptian way of death, you must have bought it for her."

"That's weak, Finn. You'll never be able—"

A noise came from the direction of the stainless-steel sarcophagus—a low, muffled sound, like a moan.

"What was that?" Kendrake said.

Greylock stared at her, wild-eyed. "What was what?"

The second time the moan was louder, accompanied by knocking.

Finn and Kendrake both bolted for the metal casket, reached it about the same time, struggled together to open it.

Inside stood a man, hands bound together behind him. His hair was matted with blood. Bleary, unfocused eyes bulged at Finn and Kendrake above a mouth sealed shut with surgical tape. He squirmed feebly.

"Canova!" Finn was no longer tipsy.

"You fools!" Greylock came up behind them, holding a revolver in both hands pointed their way. "You might have left here alive if you hadn't done that."

"Beamer's gun, I suppose," Finn said.

Greylock nodded. The gun wavered as his gaze darted between Finn and Kendrake. "We stole it. I didn't want to get it into the hands of the police until I was sure I was finished with it."

He pulled back his thumb, cocking the gun.

Kendrake, with only a slight tremor in her voice, said, "What's *he* doing here?" She indicated Canova, who wrinkled his forehead like a man with a Class A hangover.

"Another fool. I went to his house Saturday to find out how much he knew. When he made it clear that he was aware Viola had a male partner, I gave him a false description—as unlike me as possible. But apparently he wasn't satisfied with that, wanted to find out more about Viola's 'son.' So he questioned one of her neighbors and got a very different portrait."

"A man with a beard," Finn said. "And Canova thought of you." He made a mental note to give the student extra credit.

"Not right away. He came here to reconcile the two descriptions he'd heard, but before I could come up with an explanation it dawned on him that I looked like the person the neighbor described. He'd just blurted that out when I saw you two come into the building. I hit him in the head with a paperweight." Greylock indicated a heavy-looking pyramid on his desk. "I didn't expect him to wake up so soon. Now I have to deal with all of you."

He sounded put out.

Keep him talking, Finn thought. Every killer he ever knew wanted to talk about it once the game was up.

"Sorry you're having such a tough day, Greylock," he said. "Tell me, what did the arsenic in Viola's kitchen have to do with anything? You must have planted it, but I can't figure out why."

"Because I was smart. The letter Viola left with her attorney to implicate Norris guaranteed that the police would be looking for evidence she killed Norris' father. I wanted to be certain they found some. Otherwise they might continue investigating and stumble upon something that pointed my way. No one knew that digitalis was the murder weapon, so I planted arsenic. It was obviously deadly, and it was handy—I use it in my mummification formula."

Finn looked toward the sarcophagus. Canova was sweating, but his eyes were focused now—and wide open in terror.

"What did you do with Virginia Hartwell's body, the substitute corpse?" Kendrake asked.

Greylock took his left hand away from the gun and wiped it on his pants. "She's in my basement at home, soaking in wine, herbs, and chemicals. I was going to put her in that sarcophagus."

"Nice treatment for her," Finn said, "but poor Viola got the furnace."

"I didn't want it that way." Greylock's voice rose. "But she had to stipulate in her will that the body be cremated—expecting that it wouldn't really be her body." He swallowed. "I wish it hadn't been. I was fond of Viola."

"I bet," Kendrake said. "You probably got half the money she raked in from bequests and life insurance."

"I deserved it! Without my help, Viola would have been caught when she killed her second husband. Cyanide was a bad choice. I smelled bitter almonds while I was preparing his body."

"And instead of calling the cops," Finn said, "you dealt yourself in on the game. A model citizen, that's you."

"I needed the money." Greylock rested his free hand on the sarcophagus. "Just developing my mummification process was tremendously expensive. The mummy mausoleum will take millions more. I can't borrow that much."

"So the money from one murdered husband barely got you started," Finn said. "You and Viola had to kill again and again to keep the cash coming."

Kendrake edged away from Finn. "Look, Mr. Greylock, we're no danger to you. We don't have any hard evidence that could convict you. You said that yourself. All we have is the photo of Viola wearing the ankh, and that's here in my purse. I'll give it to you."

As she reached into her handbag, Greylock warned, "Don't make any sudden—"

"Joe!" a voice screamed from the doorway. It was Mary Sue Barkeloo.

Greylock spun around, quickly assessed the threat from Barkeloo as non-existent, and turned immediately back to Kendrake—who sprayed him with the chemical mace she pulled from her purse.

Greylock screamed a curse, squeezed his eyes shut, and staggered backwards.

Finn kicked the gun out of his hand.

The gun hit the floor, discharging with an ear-splitting boom.

"Hilary!" Finn yelled, looking her way.

But she was still standing, a bit dazed but unbloodied.

Greylock lunged at Finn.

Catching the movement out of the corner of his eye, Finn sprinted to one side. Kendrake stepped in, swung the stainless-steel door of the sarcophagus flat into Greylock's face. He fell on his back, unconscious, blood spurting out of his nose.

"Good work!" Finn called.

The sarcophagus, reverberating from the force of the blow to Greylock, tottered. Joe Canova, unsteady on his feet inside the metal casket, teetered—and then fell on top of Greylock.

Canova emitted a muffled scream.

"Poor man," Kendrake muttered. She rolled Canova over and ripped the tape off his mouth.

"I did it," he rasped. "I caught the son of a bitch!"

Finn slumped into Greylock's chair and called the police.

THIRTY-TWO

CLASS DISMISSED

Finn tried to stick to his scheduled lecture Wednesday night on "Locates: How to Find Anybody," but it was no use. None of the student sleuths wanted to hear it.

Everyone knew by now the general outlines of the noisy denouement at the funeral home. Both of Cincinnati's daily newspapers reported the story of Viola Beamer, murderess and murderee, in their Tuesday and Wednesday editions. The references to Finn and to the A-Plus Detective Agency were all positive, which already prompted inquiries from prospective clients and students. But the behind-the-scenes details craved by the students understandably were lacking in the press accounts.

"It was a group effort," Finn stressed, "with important contributions by Ms. Chandler, Mr. Mobarry, Funderburgh, Mrs. Pertwee, Mr. Davis, and our secretary, Mrs. Kendrake. Oh, and Mr. Canova, of course."

"And me," Barkeloo said.

"Things would have turned out very differently if Mr. Canova hadn't returned to the Eternal Rest Funeral Home, even though he found it unpleasant to do so," Finn went on, as though he didn't hear her.

Canova sat back and crossed his legs, a smug smile on his face.

"But we might all be dead if it wasn't for Ms. Barkeloo's timely entrance."

She smiled. *Pop.*

Most of the others Finn singled out were in attendance, including Kendrake. Dick Mobarry brought his scanner to show everybody. Nelson Funderburgh and Alice Pertwee—now out of the nursing home and promising never to return—arrived at class together and took adjoining seats. Shadd Davis was present only in spirit. He sent Finn a postcard from the Bucyrus (Ohio) Bratwurst Festival, where he found surprising success with a saxophone gig.

"Perhaps it would be best to begin with the events that followed our last class," Finn said. "First came Mr. Mobarry overhearing an important conversation…"

With help from each of the students involved as he told their part of the story, Finn retraced the collection of evidence, the interviews, and the wrong theories up to Kendrake's question that ultimately led her and Finn to the Eternal Rest Funeral Home shootout.

"As you probably know from the newspapers and television, Greylock recovered from his concussion and confessed everything under police interrogation."

"Good thing, huh?" Barkeloo said. *Pop.* "I mean, you didn't really have any proof against the guy, didja?"

"What do you call having the murder weapon?" Canova fired back. "Plus a body soaking in mummy juice in his basement?"

The look on Barkeloo's face suggested they'd discuss the matter later in private.

"Ms. Barkeloo actually has a good point," Finn said. "We don't know what a good defense attorney might have done if Greylock hadn't confessed to the authorities. After all, we didn't record what he admitted to us."

"Big mistake," Mobarry muttered.

"Gus Hackleshin confessed, too, by the way. He said his conscience was bothering him."

"Confessed to what?" Funderburgh asked.

"He bought stolen insulin for his diabetes from Viola Beamer at cut-rate prices. But that's a sideshow. The most important thing is that our client was exonerated."

Norris Beamer was not only free, but financially comfortable. The part of Greylock's confession dealing with the husband-murders established that Viola Beamer, as the killer, was unable to inherit from Otto Beamer or be the beneficiary of his life insurance. The son would get it all. Knowing that, Norris drew on his home equity line to pay Finn's multi-digited bill right away, allowing Finn to present his landlord with a cashier's check for the full amount owed. Cheviot Mutual was also grateful, and Calvin

Jefferson promised to throw more work to the A-Plus Detective Agency. Red Dog McCorkle made a similar pledge.

Finn had plenty of reasons then for the smile that crossed his broad face as he dismissed the class. All the cards were falling his way. Even his Maisonette dinner the night before with Becky Shanks from the Bureau of Vital Statistics worked out well; she told Finn that she was engaged. He tried to look disappointed as he congratulated her.

"Oh, Mr. Canova," Finn called. "Could you stay behind for a few moments? I have a project for you."

Canova gave a knowing grin and whispered something to Barkeloo. She hung around at the back of the classroom while the two talked.

"What's up?" Canova sucked in his gut. "Murder One?"

"Nothing that exciting, I'm afraid. It's that Hawley Smoot insurance scam again."

Canova's face fell. "But I already got the goods on that scum-bucket—on videotape, yet. And don't tell me there was anything wrong with the tape. The picture was clear enough for you to recognize the dude."

"It was a fine tape, a perfect tape, Mr. Canova. I just can't use it."

"Why the hell not?"

"Because I promised Smoot I'd destroy the tape. That's how I got him to break into Viola Beamer's house for us."

Canova's eyes bulged. "Oh, for—"

"But I didn't promise not to make a new one. If Smoot didn't take my advice to go straight, that's not my fault. You pinned him once and you can do it again, right?"

"Well, sure. But that ain't the point."

Finn reached up to put his arm around Canova. "I knew I could count on you. Think of it as experience, Mr. Canova. Every field assignment adds to your well of experience. The other students envy you."

"Yeah? Oh, yeah. I bet they do."

"Just don't rub it in."

Canova swaggered back to Barkeloo and left the building with her on his arm.

A few minutes later, Finn himself felt a glow as he surveyed his office domain with Kendrake at his side. They were in the reception area, looking around one last time before closing up for the night. The walls were patched, and the floors cleaned to a shine, thanks to a deal Kendrake cut with an out-of-work contractor. The news magazines on the coffee tables were all current. The room looked businesslike and it felt right. Almost. There was something missing, something Finn had seen lately in every kind of business from funeral home to nursing home.

"A proper office these days ought to have a computer, oughtn't it?" he said to Kendrake.

"I should say so. That's why I ordered one. The sale was still on down the street. After catching up on the rent, there was enough left in the checkbook to buy a nice PC clone."

"Why didn't you buy flowers for your desk while you were at it?"

"That would be very nice, wouldn't it? I'll stop by a florist in the morning on my way in."

"Fine." Finn was in such a good mood that he decided not to tell her that his comment had been sarcastic.

He cleared his throat. He was about to take a big gamble, and Francis Aloysius Finn was not a gambling man. "With all the new business that's been promised this agency, I feel that we need continuity here in the office. I'm afraid that a temporary secretary, while useful in an emergency, is a disadvantage on a long-term basis. I need to hire someone permanent. I had in a mind a person who can manage the office, see solutions to crimes... carry mace and use it when called for."

Kendrake smoothed her dress, a royal blue number that set off her blond hair nicely. "As it happens, I've reached a decision of my own, Mr. Finn. Working as a temporary doesn't really fulfill my personal need to be involved in something, to make a difference. I've decided to seek a permanent position... at a detective agency."

Finn opened the door. "I was hoping you'd say that, Mrs. Kendrake. Perhaps we could have a late dinner and discuss your salary."

She picked up her purse. "I'm sure we can negotiate something satisfactory."

www.ingramcontent.com/pod-product-compliance
Lightning Source LLC
Chambersburg PA
CBHW020637180626
46816CB00003B/1000